Mason wat ther, his throa eir embrace in enter.

Her brother's eyes were squeezed shut, and he hugged Karina tightly, as though this might be the last time he ever saw her. Something was going on with this kid, that's for sure.

But Karina's brother didn't want his help. And why in the world not?

When the siblings broke apart, the boy whispered something so low Mason had to strain to hear. "Don't let anything happen to my sister. Please."

Mason saw open, unmasked fear in the boy's face. An answering foreboding dropped like an icy lump into Mason's stomach in response. Then the boy was gone, leaving him alone in the sterile room with Karina, who wept quietly.

The teenager's account was a lie, no doubt about it. But he was lying because he was afraid for his sister. And that made Mason afraid for her, too.

It took all his strength not to enfold Karina in a protective embrace.

Books by Virginia Smith

Love Inspired Suspense

Murder by Mushroom
Bluegrass Peril
A Taste of Murder
Murder at Eagle Summit
Scent of Murder
Into the Deep
A Deadly Game
*Dangerous Impostor
*Bullseye

Love Inspired

A Daughter's Legacy

*Falsely Accused

VIRGINIA SMITH

A lifelong lover of books, Virginia Smith has always enjoyed immersing herself in fiction. In her mid-twenties she wrote her first story and discovered that writing well is harder than it looks; it took many years to produce a book worthy of publication. During the daylight hours, she steadily climbed the corporate ladder and stole time to write late at night after the kids were in bed. With the publication of her first novel, she left her twenty-year corporate profession to devote her energy to her passion—writing stories that honor God and bring a smile to the faces of her readers. When she isn't writing, Ginny and her husband, Ted, enjoy exploring the extremes of nature—skiing in the mountains of Utah, motorcycle riding on the curvy roads of central Kentucky and scuba diving in the warm waters of the Caribbean. Visit her online at www.virginiasmith.org.

BULLSEYE

VIRGINIA SMITH

Love Inspired

Recycling programs
for this product may
not exist in your area.

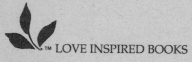

™ LOVE INSPIRED BOOKS

ISBN-13: 978-0-373-67517-3

BULLSEYE

www.LoveInspiredBooks.com

Printed in U.S.A.

Therefore confess your sins to each other
and pray for each other so that you may be healed.
The prayer of a righteous person
is powerful and effective.
—*James* 5:16

ONE

Loud pounding from somewhere nearby reached into Karina Guerrero's dream and dragged her to wakefulness. Heart thudding in sync with the beats, she forced her eyes open. Darkness blurred the corners of her bedroom like sleep blurred her thoughts. Those guys in the apartment next door hadn't ever been this noisy.

Bang, bang, bang.

"Albuquerque police department. Open up!"

The voice, deeply male and harshly insistent, chased away the last tendrils of sleep. The police— here? Not an annoying stereo after all. She forced her eyes to focus on the clock on the nightstand. Three thirty-seven in the morning. Fear, sharp as a knife's blade, sliced through her insides. Had something happened to Alex?

"I'm coming."

Her voice, squeaky with panic, filled the apartment as she jerked on a pair of sweatpants and a T-shirt over her pajamas. No time to brush her sleep-tousled hair, so she pulled the thick dark mass into a messy knot at the back of her neck as she hurried across the tiny living room to the front door. A quick peek through the peephole settled her fear deeper inside. A stern-faced man with short-cropped hair frowned at her from the sidewalk outside.

Please don't let something have happened to Alex.

She unlocked the door and opened it. Not just one officer, but two. Both men. Surely if they were coming to give her bad news, they would have sent a woman, right? She grasped at the thought and could not find a voice for the question that screamed in her mind.

"Hello, Karina," the first officer said.

The familiar use of her name made her look more closely at him. A face from the past peered back at her.

"Parker Harding." She hadn't thought about him in several years. Memories of him inevitably brought back memories of his friend and former partner, and she absolutely could *not* allow herself to think of Mason Sinclair. That was too painful.

The shadowy smile hovering around Parker's mouth acknowledged the painful memories, but thankfully he didn't bring up old times. Instead, he gestured toward the man standing beside him. "This is my partner, Officer Graham. We're sorry to disturb you at such a late hour, but we're hoping you can help us."

A flicker of hope sparked to life. That didn't sound like someone bringing bad news. Maybe something had happened in the neighborhood, and they were checking for witnesses. That wouldn't be unusual in this apartment complex. She nodded, still unable to speak.

He held her gaze as he spoke. "We're looking for Alex, Karina. Our records indicate he lives here with you."

His words landed like slaps across her face. Alex must be in some kind of trouble.

He said lives, not lived. That means he's alive. Right?

Fingers biting into the flesh of her arms, she managed to find her voice. "Is he in some kind of trouble?" She swallowed. "Is he okay?"

Did she imagine it, or did Parker's expression soften just a fraction? And if it did, was it with pity?

"Karina, it's very important that we talk to your brother. Is he at home?"

"No, he's not. He's staying the night with a friend. I can give you the address."

Parker exchanged a glance with his partner. "Is his friend's name José Garcia?"

Oh no. Was José in trouble, then? The times Karina had met him he'd seemed like a good kid. "Yes, that's right."

Officer Graham's expression grew grim. "José Garcia was killed tonight, ma'am. Several witnesses saw him with your brother right before the shooting. That's why we need to speak with Alexander."

A wave of shock washed over her, leaving her

dizzy. She clutched at the door to keep from falling. José dead? But he was only fourteen years old. And where was Alex?

"I—" She swallowed, trying to put life into her numb tongue. "I don't know where Alex is. He was spending the night at José's. Have you looked there?"

José's parents will be devastated!

"Mr. and Mrs. Garcia haven't seen him." Officer Graham straightened and assumed an authoritative stance. "Ms. Guerrero, we'd like permission to look in Alexander's room. Will you allow us to do that?"

"But I already told you, he's not here." Wait a minute. Why did they want to look in Alex's room? She clutched the edge of the heavy wooden door and peered up into Parker's face. "Parker, surely you don't think Alex would do anything to hurt José. You remember Alex, right? My brother is a good boy. He goes to school, gets good grades. He even has a job and helps pay our bills."

His answer confirmed her suspicions.

"Karina, we need to take a look. If we need to get a warrant to search Alexander's room, we can have it within fifteen minutes."

Karina opened her mouth to insist that Alex wouldn't do anything wrong. In a city where teenagers ran in gangs and did drugs and robbed convenience stores, fourteen-year-old Alex was an anomaly. He was polite and helpful and responsible. But she kept her arguments to herself. These men were doing their job, but their job chilled the blood in her veins.

If Alex wasn't at José's house, and if José was dead, then where was her brother? Let them look in his room. They'd find nothing, because there was nothing to find. Then maybe they'd realize that the kid they were looking for wasn't running from them—he was missing, Probably frightened, and maybe even hurt.

Without a word, she swung the door open wider to invite them inside. They followed her across the living room and down the short hallway past the bathroom she and her brother shared. Alex's door was closed, as always when he wasn't there. She twisted the knob, threw it open and flipped the light switch.

And froze, stunned.

There, crouched in the corner between his dresser and closet door, was Alex. His clothes were covered in blood.

Mason Sinclair bit into his toast and examined his schedule for the day. His lone client at the moment would arrive at his office at one o'clock this afternoon to hear a report of his wife's infidelity, complete with pictures. Lots of them.

"Poor slob," Mason mumbled.

A loud snore drifted down the hallway from the direction of the second bedroom. His roommate, Caleb. Six months ago Caleb had moved from Las Vegas to Atlanta at Mason's suggestion. Along with their friend Brent, the three formed the Falsely Accused Support Team to help prove the innocence of people who'd been accused of crimes they didn't commit. Since they began, F.A.S.T. had helped clear four innocent people.

Mason took pride in their success rate. He enjoyed helping people who were in the same tight spot he'd been in four years ago. Only he didn't have a F.A.S.T. team to help him, so he'd faced the accusations alone.

His cell phone interrupted his thoughts. He swallowed another gulp of coffee, then leaned back in his chair to grab the phone from the kitchen counter by the tail of its charger. An unfamiliar number appeared on the screen. 505 area code. He knew without looking it up where that was. Albuquerque. The thought was enough to make him put the phone back on the counter and ignore the call. There wasn't a single person in Albuquerque he wanted to talk to.

After a few rings the call went to voice mail. He waited for the chime telling him he had received a new message. Instead the phone rang again. Same phone number. Somebody really wanted to talk to him. Must be important.

Before he could second-guess his decision, he answered the call. "Hello?"

A sharp intake of breath, then a female voice said, "Mason?"

At the familiar tone, memories engulfed him. Gone were the kitchen and the open jar of grape jelly on the table in front of him. Forgotten were his notebook and coffee mug. Instead, vivid images rose in his mind. Picnics on the grass. Hikes in the Sandia Mountains. Wavy black hair blown by a hot desert breeze. More vivid than the images were the feelings. Sweet lips moving against his. Soft arms wrapped around his neck. And something else.

Guilt.

Primarily he felt the sick bite of guilt gnawing in his gut. Just like always.

He wrapped the fingers of one hand around his coffee mug and squeezed. "Been a long time, Karina."

Another breath sounded through the phone line, this one shaky. "I called because I need help, Mason. I wouldn't ask except I don't have anyone else. We're alone."

Several questions came to mind, but he asked the obvious one first. "We?"

"Alex and me. My dad passed away two years ago."

More memories. Nine-year-old Alex playing volleyball with Mason at a church-sponsored picnic, while Mr. Guerrero and Karina sat on the sidelines cheering them on. Karina cheered louder for him than for Alex.

Mason leaned forward and pushed the coffee mug toward the center of the table. "I didn't know. I'm sorry."

"Mason, Alex is in trouble and I don't know what to do."

Alex would be about fourteen now, a teenager. "What's he gotten into?"

"He's being held in the juvenile detention center. They've charged him with murder. But he didn't do it. I promise he didn't."

Mason sat back against the wooden spindles of his chair. Murder. The word fell on his ears like a gong, resonating with horrible feelings from his own past.

A movement drew his attention to the hallway. Caleb stumbled out of his bedroom, lumbered into the kitchen and headed straight for the coffee pot. The big man's hair, normally caught back in a ponytail, hung in tangles after a night of fighting with his pillow.

Mason flapped a hand in his direction to keep him quiet, and said into the phone, "Who do they say he murdered?"

That got Caleb's attention. He whirled around, coffee carafe still in hand, and peered intently at Mason.

"A friend. José Garcia." Her voice held a sob. "He was only fourteen, like Alex."

He flipped to the back of his notebook, found a blank page and jotted down the victim's name. He'd see what he could find out later. Caleb moved closer to read over his shoulder, so beside the name he wrote *14 years old* and underlined it. Caleb winced.

"Does Alex have an attorney?"

"Not yet. I can't afford to hire one, so he'll have a public defender assigned. But it's been two days, and so far we haven't heard anything. The court wasn't open over the weekend."

Mason wrote *public defender* beneath the victim's name and exchanged a glance with Caleb. There were some really good public defenders out there, but most were inexperienced and young in their legal careers, trying to build a résumé.

"We need you, Mason. Alex needs you." Karina's tone became a plea. "Can you come to New Mexico and help us?"

Before he could stop it, a laugh burst out in a blast. Him, go to Albuquerque? What a suggestion. "Hold on there. I can't just drop everything and hop on a plane. I have a business to run here in Atlanta." Albuquerque? No way. Never again.

Caleb slid into the empty chair on the other side of the dinette table and raised his eyebrows. Mason glared at him.

"But I thought that's what you do these days, help people who are accused of a crime they didn't commit."

That made him squirm in his chair. Where did she hear about the Falsely Accused Support Team? Probably that website Brent had insisted on building. They'd gotten dozens of inquiries and several clients since he'd launched it.

"Listen, we're in Atlanta. Our connections, our contacts, are here." Never mind that their first case, the one that spawned F.A.S.T., had occurred in Vegas. The whole team lived here now, and that's where they concentrated their efforts.

"You have contacts in Albuquerque," she shot back, her voice full of the old fire he remembered so well. He used to tease her about her hot Latin temper.

"Not anymore." He closed his eyes against a wave of emotion. His so-called contacts in New Mexico were all four years old. He'd shut off that part of his life, separated it in a sealed compartment that he never wanted to open.

"Please, Mason. I have nowhere else to turn."

Part of him wanted so badly to help her. He owed it to her, to make up for all the pain he'd inflicted on her in the past. But he had pain too, didn't he? Going back to Albuquerque, the source of the memories that haunted his dreams, wasn't something he was willing to do.

And yet, there's still a killer on the loose there. He probably gloats over the fact that he killed my wife four years ago and went scot-free.

Mason raised his free hand and massaged his temples with a thumb and finger. Not his problem. Not anymore.

He spoke softly. "Karina, I can't."

She was sobbing openly now. "You mean you won't. You won't help me. Alex will go to prison, and you won't lift a finger."

The accusation writhed in his chest. He couldn't argue, because it was true. He opened his mouth to say "I'm sorry," but she had already hung up.

Mason set his cell phone beside his unfinished breakfast and closed his notebook.

From across the table Caleb studied him through narrowed eyes. "What was that all about?"

"I don't want to talk about it." Mason picked up his half-eaten toast and wadded it inside a napkin.

"Sounded like a F.A.S.T. client from this end of the conversation."

"Nope."

"Then what were you saying about—"

"Drop it." Mason loaded the words with warning.

Caleb lifted his head and spoke toward the ceiling. "Lord, please help my Brother to heal from whatever is causing him to be such a jerk."

Oh, for cryin' out loud. This habit of praying at the drop of a hat was really starting to get to him. Mason stood, snatched up his mug and slung cooled coffee into the sink. "If you must pray, there's a closet in your room."

He might as well not have spoken. Caleb ignored him. "If that was a F.A.S.T. call, then you just turned down a new client without even consulting the rest of us."

Mason dropped into his chair and heaved an exasperated sigh. "It wasn't a new client. It was an old friend."

The big man's eyebrows rose. "You turned down an old friend?"

"Oh, for Pete's sake!" Caleb wasn't going to let this go until he needled the information out of him. "All right, here's the scoop. An old girlfriend's kid brother has gotten into trouble. He's facing a murder rap, and she swears he's innocent. Wants me to drop everything and hop a plane to Albuquerque." He forced a hollow-sounding laugh. "That's messed up, isn't it?"

Caleb's brows creased as he thought. "Do you think the boy did it?"

"How would I know? I haven't seen him in four

years." An image of a skinny, dark haired Hispanic boy with oversized front teeth rose in his mind. "He used to be a good kid," he admitted, "but a lot can change between ten and fourteen years old."

"What about your girlfriend?" Caleb's deep voice became soft. "Can you trust her judgment?"

"She's not my girlfriend." The words fired across his tongue like bullets leaving a 357. "She's my ex-fiancée." He snapped his mouth shut. Great. Now he'd busted open the vault, and exposed a glimpse of his ugly past.

"Aha." The big man rubbed his hands together and leaned forward. "Now we're getting somewhere. This isn't just a simple case. It's a matter of the heart."

"You're wrong. I have no heart."

The big man's laughter filled the small room. "Oh, you have a heart all right. It's hard as granite, but it's there. And if you ask me, you have a soft spot in there for Karina and her kid brother. Deep down, you want to help them. The only reason you said no is because you're afraid."

Now it was Mason's turn to laugh. "That's ridiculous. Afraid of what?"

Caleb's answer was agonizingly soft. "Ghosts."

A twist in the vicinity of Mason's chest affirmed the truth. He *was* afraid of ghosts. Not his deceased wife's. The ghosts that haunted him from Albuquerque were harsh, ugly and painful. The heartbreak of loss. The agony of loneliness. The guilt of the pain he'd caused Karina.

And the ghost of a killer who still walked the streets.

"Some ghosts need to be confronted." Caleb leaned forward and rested his arms on his thighs. "Otherwise they never stop haunting."

Much as he hated to admit it, Mason knew his friend was right. It was time.

TWO

Karina blotted tears from her eyes and tossed the damp tissue into the wastebasket with the others. It had taken every ounce of courage she could muster to make that phone call to Mason. Did he have any idea how hard it was for her to ask for help?

Red numbers glowed from the face of the DVD player in her small entertainment center. Almost seven o'clock Monday morning. If she was going to work, she should be dressed and ready to go. She held out a hand and watched her fingers tremble. Nobody would trust her with a pair of sharp shears near their heads today. How could she cut hair when Alex had been in juvy—the nickname for the juvenile justice center—for over forty-eight hours, and she was no closer to getting him out?

She snatched another tissue from the box when a fresh onslaught of tears threatened. Asking Mason for help had been a long shot anyway. Of course he wouldn't help *her,* but she thought maybe he would consider helping Alex. They'd been buddies back before… Her mind skirted over the miserable weeks that had marked the end of her engagement.

Maybe if Mason had stayed with her, Alex wouldn't be in this mess now. He would have had a strong role model to look up to after their father had passed away. He wouldn't have gotten involved with…

With what? What had Alex gotten into? Was he involved in drugs and gangs, as the police said? And if so, how had she missed the signs?

Karina paced into the kitchen and poured cold coffee into a mug. Day-old coffee didn't sound appealing, but she had to do something with her hands or she might start pulling her hair out. She set the mug in the microwave, punched a button and watched as the mug revolved inside. A sob threatened, but she choked it back before it could escape.

Okay. She had to get hold of herself, clear her mind. Sitting around the apartment crying wouldn't help Alex. She had to do something. But what? Since Mason wouldn't help her, who would?

A lawyer? She'd told Mason the truth when she'd said she couldn't afford to hire an attorney. A hair stylist with custody of a teenager didn't have a lot of extra money for things like lawyers. Sometimes she barely had enough to keep the lights on. She would gladly take out a loan to pay for a top-notch attorney, but she had nothing to use as collateral. Her car was worth less than she owed and she rented her apartment. So that meant Alex would have a public defender assigned, and all she could do was pray that it would be a good one.

But it might be several days before he got a lawyer. The officer at juvy had told her the court's dockets were usually booked solid early in the week, so it could be Tuesday or even later before the judge reviewed Alex's case.

The microwave beeped and shut off. Well, that was one thing she could do. She could be waiting at the juvenile justice center when the offices opened, and demand that her brother's case be reviewed today. It might not do any good, but it was something.

With the decision came a sense of purpose. Anything was better than sitting around the apartment crying. She opened the microwave door and dumped the steaming stale coffee in the sink, then headed toward her bedroom. A dress would make her look more professional than slacks, and she'd tame her thick mass of hair back into something respectable looking. If she could make a good impression on the judge, maybe he would give Alex the best free lawyer available.

Her phone rang, and she altered her path to retrieve it from the sofa where she'd dropped it. A glance at the screen stopped her in her tracks. Mason's number.

"Mason?" She hated the way her voice quivered when she spoke his name.

"I've changed my mind." His words were clipped, abrupt. "I'll be there tomorrow morning. Pick me up at the airport at nine-fifteen."

The line went dead.

Hope inflated like a balloon in her chest and crowded the breath from her lungs. Mason was coming. But why? She stared at the receiver in her hand. What changed his mind? It couldn't have anything to do with her. She was bitterly certain of that. He must have reconsidered because of Alex.

"Gracias a Dios," she whispered. Help for any reason was better than no help at all.

Her step lighter, she turned once again toward the bedroom. A sight outside her living room window stopped her. A dark car was parked there, longways in the parking lot, blocking her little red Toyota sedan. The driver's door stood open, and a man stood on the pavement, his muscular arms folded across the hood. He didn't move, but stood still, facing her way. Though his eyes were concealed by dark sunglasses, Karina felt intensity in the gaze turned toward her front window. Toward her.

A glance at the doorknob showed the lock engaged, the deadbolt in place. Drawn by a sort of horrified fascination, she inched closer to the window. Could he see her through the blinds?

With one finger she pushed down on one of the metal slats and bent it to get a better look at him. When she did, she felt those invisible eyes fixed on her. An icy chill slid up her spine.

The man's head dipped once, as though acknowledging her. Then he slid into the car, slammed the door and sped away.

It was a long time before Karina managed to lift a fear-numbed hand and screw the blinds tightly shut.

THREE

The nonstop flight from Atlanta to Albuquerque lasted over three and a half hours, plenty of time for Mason to regret his change of heart. Actually he'd regretted it thirty seconds after he'd hung up from Karina yesterday, but Caleb had refused to let him call back and rescind the offer of help. To make matters worse, Caleb had called Brent, the third member of F.A.S.T., to come over last night to help badger him. No amount of protesting on Mason's part had made a difference. Lauren, Brent's wealthy wife, even rebuffed his claims that he couldn't afford the trip and insisted on picking up the tab for the pro bono work. Some friends they were.

On top of everything else the only seat available on the flight at the last minute was in the middle, between a talkative woman on her way to visit her grandson—with the pictures to prove it—and a sleeping businessman who snored the whole time. The plane bounced its way through choppy air during the last hour of the flight and Mason spilled coffee on his white shirt.

So when he exited the aircraft at Albuquerque International, he was already in a foul mood. He scanned the crowd waiting outside of the security gate. If Karina wasn't here, he'd march straight over to the ticket counter and use his credit card to book a same-day ticket back home. He halfway hoped she wouldn't show.

A waving hand snagged his gaze. Beneath the slender arm he caught sight of a familiar face framed by a shining mass of thick, black hair.

He nearly dropped his carry-on bag. The woman *looked* like Karina, but when had she become so gorgeous?

His feet must have kept moving, because in the next moment he was standing in front of her, searching the beautiful face turned up to his. Though she'd matured into a stunning woman, she was the same old Karina. Same dark eyes. Same adorable nose. Same full lips. He swallowed against a throat gone dry with the sudden assault of the memory of those lips on his.

Tears glistened in her eyes. "Thank you for coming, Mason."

He meant to say "You're welcome." When he opened his mouth, those were the words his brain instructed his tongue to speak. Instead, out came a sarcastic quip, fueled by the stirring of unwelcome feelings. "I had nothing important planned for the next few days anyway."

The tears dried in an instant. Those soft lips tightened, and her shoulders stiffened. "Meaning Alex and I are not important?" Anger made her voice sharp.

Oops. Not what he meant at all. Why in the world did he always speak before he thought? On the other hand, what did she expect? An open-armed reception, as if the past four years had never happened? As if Margie had never happened?

But that wasn't her fault.

He softened his tone. "I'm sorry. It's just that there are a lot of memories here, you know?"

The anger melted off her face, replaced with a gentle gaze that was much harder to take. "I know."

The tenderness in her tone stirred up uncomfortable feelings in him. The only way he could handle returning to the place where Margie died was by donning a thick layer of sarcasm and indifference. But the one person who could always cut through that armor was standing in front of him.

He glanced at the escalator. The ticket counters were one floor up. All he had to do was whip out a credit card and blow this place. Coming here was a bad idea yesterday, and it was still a bad idea today. No matter what Caleb said, sometimes it was best to leave the ghosts in their graves.

Karina followed his gaze and her arms rose to wrap around her middle. He recognized the gesture from years ago. Whenever she was upset, or insecure, or frightened, that's what she did.

An emotion he preferred to ignore stirred him at

the sight. With a final glance toward the escalator, he shouldered his carry-on bag.

"How soon can you get me in to talk to Alex?"

When they brought Alex into the visitation room at the juvenile justice center, Mason got his second shock of the day. The ten-year-old kid had grown into his oversized teeth. Alex was a hulking teenager, a couple of inches taller than Mason's five-ten and a good ten pounds heavier than him. It was almost impossible to see the skinny kid in this slightly chunky young man, except for a strong resemblance to his petite older sister.

"Alex, you've grown up," Mason managed as they shook hands.

"Yes, sir."

He stooped to hug Karina, who embraced her brother with obvious emotion. "How are you, baby? Are you eating? Is the food good here?"

Alex held on to her for a long moment, then released her. "It's okay."

He dropped into a molded plastic orange chair, one of four in an otherwise empty visiting room. Karina scooted another one near, so she could sit close. Mason dragged a third chair away from the wall and positioned it so he could face both of them. On the other side of the long glass half-wall a guard sat behind a high counter watching with a dispassionate expression. When Alex reached over and grabbed his sister's hand, Mason's heart warmed. The kid who adored his big sister was still in there.

"Alex, Mason flew here from Atlanta to help us." Karina flashed a hopeful smile toward Mason. "He's a private investigator now, so he knows how to find proof that you didn't kill José."

The news had a surprising impact on the kid. His eyes widened for a moment as he looked at Mason, then his brows dropped into a frown. He released his sister's hand, folded his arms across his chest and scooted down in his seat, the picture of a sullen teenager.

"I don't need anybody's help. I told you, I'll be fine."

Interesting. Mason studied his body language. Closed up tight, just like his sister. Probably for the same reason, to protect himself from vulnerability. Only Mason detected a hint of something else in the way the kid's chin dropped and his shoulders hunched forward. He knew enough about body language to recognize that Alex was afraid of something. But what?

"Yes, you do." Karina slipped a hand inside the kid's arm and gave it a gentle tug. "Mason has experience with people who are charged with crimes they didn't commit, just like you."

Mason folded one leg across the other and asked casually, "You didn't do it, did you?"

Alex didn't quite meet his eyes. "No. But I'm gonna get a lawyer, and he'll prove it."

"That's great. But since I came all the way from Atlanta would you at least tell me what happened?" He leaned back in his chair and waited.

Alex stared at the floor, considering. Karina drew a breath to speak, but Mason warned her with a glance to keep quiet. Something was going on with this kid, and he didn't want to push him too hard.

"Okay. I guess." He looked up, but his gaze still didn't connect with Mason's. "Me and my friend José were hanging out, you know? We weren't doing nothing wrong." He glanced sideways at Karina. "We should have stayed at José's house, like we were supposed to, but we got bored. So we were walking and talking, and we were cutting through this alley when a guy jumps out and points a gun at us. He wanted money, but we told the guy we don't have any, and he starts yelling at us, like, 'I know you do. Hand it over.'"

Karina looked startled. She glanced at Mason, an unreadable message in her eyes, but kept quiet. He made a mental note to ask her later.

"Go on," he urged.

"The next thing I knew, there was a shot, and José fell backward on the ground. I was standing there, looking at him, when the guy shoved the gun in my hand and took off." Alex finally looked up, and held Mason's gaze. "I didn't kill José. Honest."

That was the first truthful comment out of the boy's mouth. Mason had studied interrogation techniques, and he felt sure everything Alex had said up until now was a lie. Oh, there might be a shred of truth in there somewhere, but it was buried pretty deep.

"And the blood on your clothes?" he asked, careful to keep any hint of suspicion out of his voice.

"José's. He was still alive." Tears glimmered in his eyes. "He was crying, *help me, help me.* I tried to pick him up, to carry him out of that alley to get help, but—" his throat moved as he swallowed "—he died."

Agony sounded in Alex's tortured voice. How well Mason recognized that emotion. He leaned forward and placed a hand briefly on the boy's knee. "I'm sorry. I know how hard that must have been."

Karina sniffed and wiped her eyes with a hand. "And then you came home?"

He nodded. "I didn't know where else to go. I should have stayed there and called 911, but I was scared." He averted his gaze again, and leaned back slightly in his chair, away from Mason and Karina both. "But you don't have to worry about me. I'll work it out."

Mason started to ask how Alex planned to work things out from jail without help, but Karina beat him to it. "How can you say that? You're in juvy. You need help from anyone who will give it to you."

"I don't need any help." Alex's shout echoed off the visitation room's bare walls. "You need to just stay out of it. Mind your own business."

Karina reeled backward as if slapped. Blood

drained from her cheeks. "But we're family, Alex. Whatever happens to you happens to me."

The boy leaned sideways and gathered Karina in his arms. Mason's first instinct was to jump between them, to protect Karina from this kid who obviously was having some temper problems and therefore couldn't be trusted. But the tender expression on Alex's face as he hugged his sister stopped him. There was an ocean full of emotion on the boy's face, all open for him to see. Worry. Fear. Anxiety. But primarily love. No doubt at all that he loved Karina as much as she loved him.

Then he released her and lumbered to his feet. "I think the time's about over."

Karina looked at her watch and protested. "We still have a few minutes."

But Alex had already crossed the room in three long-legged steps and banged on the door. The guard standing outside opened it instantly.

"Wait!" Karina hurried to the door to give Alex one last hug. "I'll be back tomorrow. Take care of yourself. Eat all your vegetables."

Mason followed at a slower pace, his throat oddly constricted as he watched their embrace. Alex's eyes were squeezed shut, and he hugged Karina tightly, as though this might be the last time he ever saw her. *Something's going on with this kid, that's for sure.* And now that Mason had seen him again, he wanted to find out more.

But obviously Alex didn't want his help. And why in the world not?

When they broke apart, Mason extended his hand. "I'll come with her to see you again, if that's okay." He shrugged and grinned. "Might as well. I'm in town for a few days anyway."

Alex took his hand, but to his great surprise, he pulled him into an embrace. Mason wasn't sure how to react as the boy's free arm rose and thumped him affectionately on the back. But when his mouth drew close to Mason's ear, he whispered something so low Mason had to strain to hear.

"Don't let anything happen to my sister. Please."

When Alex pulled away, Mason saw open, unmasked fear in his face. An answering foreboding dropped like an icy lump into Mason's stomach in response. Then Alex was gone, leaving him alone in the sterile room with Karina, who wept quietly.

Alex's account was a lie, no doubt about it. But he was lying because he was afraid for his sister. And that made Mason afraid for her, too.

It took all his strength not to enfold her in a protective embrace.

FOUR

Karina stood beside the metal detector near the front
guard's desk, waiting for her purse and identification
to be returned to her and trying hard to maintain an
appearance of pleasant composure. Behind the mask
the mercury in her temper's thermometer was climb-
ing upward. What was the matter with Alex? He'd
never raised his voice to her before, not once. All his
life he'd been an easygoing, cooperative kid. Now all
of a sudden when he needed help in the worst kind
of way, he turned into a stereotypical teenager, surly
and stubborn.

Of course being in jail had to be wearing on him.
He'd always been quiet, even a little shy, and had
never been in any trouble. It must be hard, being confined with juvenile delinquents. She glanced around
the tiny entry room at the painted concrete walls,
the video camera suspended from the ceiling in the
corner pointed in her direction, the high counter and
thick safety glass embedded with wire mesh behind
which the guards sat. No telling what kind of violent

kids were in this place. Alex probably had to assume a fake tough-guy persona just to survive.

She pushed the thought away. If she spent time thinking of her baby brother at the mercy of hardened criminals and violent gang members, she'd lose her mind.

She turned her head toward Mason, who stood beside her. "I don't understand why he said—"

He cut her off with a raised hand, a look of warning on his face. His eyes moved toward the uniformed guard seated behind the counter, and then back to her.

Karina snapped her mouth shut. Of course Mason was right. Anything they said could be overheard and potentially used against Alex. But for some reason the commanding expression on Mason's face irritated her even further, and she had to clamp her teeth together in order to hold back a heated reply.

She'd been so relieved when Mason had agreed to come to Albuquerque and help her. But from the moment she saw him in the airport, she'd regretted her decision to call him. When had he become so sarcastic, his manner so biting? She'd watched him descend the escalator toward the baggage claim area, his eyes darting all around as if he was planning an escape route. She'd always been able to gauge his thoughts by his expression, and that ability had not faded in the years since he broke off their engagement. He was sorry he'd come, and given an opportunity, he'd board the next plane to Atlanta in half a heartbeat.

The female guard returned to the window with her

purse and slid it, along with their drivers' licenses, through the metal tray opening in the window. Karina snatched the purse and license, and left Mason to retrieve his own.

"Thank you."

His voice and his wide smile toward the officer were overly polite, in her opinion. That irritated her even further.

She managed to hold her tongue until they stepped outside into the bright sunshine. Then she snapped, "Don't tell me what to do, Mason."

He looked surprised. "What are you talking about?"

Her pointy heels stomped the pavement a little harder than she intended as she marched toward her car. "You shushed me in there."

His mouth opened to protest, but he stopped, nodded. "All right, I did. But you've got to remember that anything overheard during a visitation can be used in court."

"I know that." She clamped her lips shut. Why was she being so foul-tempered? He really was only trying to help. She slowed her step a fraction and drew in a slow breath. "I do know that," she said more calmly. "And I definitely don't want to do anything that could hurt Alex. What I started to say is I don't know why he told the mugger they didn't have any money."

His eyebrows rose a fraction. "Did he have any?"

She nodded. "Two hundred dollars. The detention center gave it to me with the rest of his stuff after he was brought here. If he'd just handed over the money, José might not be dead now."

They reached her car parked halfway across the parking lot. Mason stopped beside the passenger door while she rounded the front bumper toward the driver's side. She pressed the unlock button on the keyless entry and heard the locks click open, but Mason made no move to get inside. Instead he watched her across the roof of the car, a measuring expression on his face.

"What?" she asked. "Why are you looking like that?"

"Karina, how truthful is Alex?" She drew a breath to jump to her brother's defense. He was a good kid and he didn't lie. But Mason stopped her with a raised hand. "I know what you're going to say, and before you do, I want you to know he lied through almost that whole visit."

Hot anger surged. How dare he waltz in here after being gone for so long and accuse her brother of dishonesty? "He did not!"

A long-suffering expression settled over Mason's features. "Karina, if you're going to argue with every word I say, why did you call me for help?"

"Well, maybe I shouldn't have," she fired back.

"Fine." A touch of temper in his voice gave the word volume. "Take me back to the airport right now and I'll go home."

His glare across the roof of the car served to clear her head. Though part of her wanted nothing more than to drive him straight back to the airport, a bigger part was terrified to see him go. Irritating though he might be, Mason was the only person she knew who could help clear Alex of this accusation. After all, he had been in nearly the same situation a few years ago.

That thought doused the fires of her anger completely. Returning to Albuquerque must be really hard for Mason. Not only had his wife been murdered after only a few months of marriage, but he'd been accused of the crime. Just driving through the city must stir up some horribly painful memories. No wonder he was so bad tempered.

With an effort, she softened her voice. "I'm sorry." She had to force the words out, but at least she said them. "I don't want you to leave. But I do need you to believe that Alex didn't kill José."

Her words had the desired effect. The hard expression softened, and when he spoke the sharp edge in his voice had dulled. "I don't think he did. But I've studied interrogation techniques, and his body language gave him away in there. He lied about what he and José were doing on the streets that night, and about how José was killed. Why would he lie?"

"I don't know." A memory arose from deep inside the twisted knot in her stomach. Alex cowering in the corner of his bedroom, his entire body trembling, his eyes round as hubcaps. "But you should have seen him that night, Mason. He was terrified."

Something flashed across Mason's countenance, an unreadable expression that was slightly alarming in the intensity with which he searched her face across the hot metal of the car's roof.

Then his eyes moved as his gaze slid sideways to fix on something behind her. His brows gathered together beneath deep creases in his forehead.

"Is that a friend of yours over there?"

She turned her head to follow his gaze.

Her chest squeezed tight around her suddenly thudding heart. It was the same dark car that had been parked outside her apartment yesterday morning. A muscular arm lay casually across the open window, and the same man stared at her through dark sunglasses. Once again, the invisible gaze felt heavy with menace.

She gasped. "That's him! That's the man who was outside my apartment yesterday." She jerked her car door open, her instincts telling her that the best course of action was to jump inside and lock the doors.

On the other side of the car, Mason straightened. Without hesitating he headed toward the dark car with a long-legged, determined stride.

Before he'd taken three steps, the car sped away.

FIVE

Mason snapped his seatbelt into place and tried not to glare at Karina. "Why didn't you tell me on the phone that someone was watching your apartment?"

He tried to tame his tone, but judging by the way her dark eyes snapped sideways at him as she turned the key in the ignition, he didn't do a very good job.

"Because I didn't see him until after we hung up. And you were so abrupt and rude on the phone I wasn't about to call you back." The engine roared to life with an excess of gasoline from the force of her foot on the pedal.

She has a point. I probably wasn't very nice to her.

But what did she expect after practically coercing him into coming back here, to the place where memories stabbed at him like poisoned darts? Everywhere he went in this town, ugly reminders would rise to taunt him with his failures. His broken engagement. The pain and betrayal in Karina's face when he told her he was in love with someone else. His brief marriage, and of course, his dead wife.

Not Karina's fault. She was the victim in our re-

lationship, an innocent bystander who got her heart broken. By me.

He turned his head to stare through the windshield. That, of course, made things a hundred times worse. He'd much rather be the dumpee than the dumper. Living with the aftermath was easier.

She steered the car from the parking lot onto Second Street. The black sedan was nowhere in sight, not that he would have followed the guy anyway. Not with Karina in the car. Coming so closely on the heels of Alex's request to protect his sister, the man's presence had served to emphasize that there was a real need. A real danger.

Why hadn't he been quick enough to note the license plate number before the car sped off? All he had to go on was that it was a black Chevy Impala, probably an '07 or an '08, and how many thousands of those were there in Albuquerque?

"Turn left up here." He pointed toward an upcoming intersection. She gave him a questioning glance, but he went on before she could ask. "I found out something else you neglected to tell me. Why didn't you tell me the name of the investigating officer?"

He'd made a phone call yesterday, the conversation fully as painful as he'd expected. But there was only one person in all of New Mexico that he could still trust, and that was Parker Harding, his former partner on the police force and the man who'd been his primary support in the aftermath of Margie's death.

Talking to him was like prying open an old wound with a tire iron.

Karina's shoulders sagged, and she avoided his gaze. "I didn't know how much to tell you. I knew how…unpleasant coming here would be for you. I was afraid to scare you off before you even got here."

"Hmm." Unpleasant. Well, that was the understatement of the century. "Turn right on Griegos and head for Rio Grande Boulevard."

She switched on her turn signal, glanced back and changed lanes. "Where are we going?"

"I warned you on the phone all my contacts are four years old, but we've got to start somewhere. I gave Parker a call last night to let him know I'd be in town. He's expecting us."

He hadn't seen his former partner and best friend since he put the nightmare of Margie's death behind him and high-tailed it out of New Mexico. Mason felt a little guilty about that, because Parker had been staunchly supportive even during the hardest parts of the ordeal, when the newspaper headlines and television newscasters were daily convicting him of killing his wife. But the plain truth was when Mason crossed the Georgia state line, he left *everything* behind. Every painful part of his past, including his friends.

No doubt the first few minutes of their reunion would be tough, with the inevitable platitudes about the passage of time and questions about how he was doing. If he could manage to make it through those first awkward moments, then maybe he'd learn something that could help him clear Alex before anyone got hurt. Especially Karina.

Four years sat heavy on Parker. When he opened the front door of his home, Mason couldn't help but notice that his old partner was thicker around the middle than he used to be, and a sprinkling of gray decorated the temples of his military-style haircut. The same ready grin broke free on his face, though.

"Hey, buddy!" Before he knew what was happening, Mason was caught up in a hearty embrace, his back thumped enthusiastically. "It's been a long time, way too long."

It took Mason only a moment to recover from his surprise and return the hug. Thankfully the display ended before things got awkward. Parker released him, and his features became solemn.

Mason braced himself. *Here it comes.*

"So, how are you doing?" Parker asked, his voice loaded with unspoken meaning. "Are you okay?"

No doubt what he was referring to. Long-ignored memories buzzed around Mason's brain like a swarm of killer bees. The unexpected knock on the apartment door in the late afternoon. Chuckling to himself, thinking Margie had forgotten her house key again. Finding Parker on his doorstep, his expression tormented. The terrible news falling from his lips like blows against Mason's heart. *Sarge called, thought I should be the one to tell you...Margie's been shot...*

head wound...ambulance...didn't survive... Shock
had rendered him numb, the words nonsense. But
Parker's expression had been impossible to escape.
Or to forget. The grief, the agony, the compassion.

Mason steeled himself, forced a smile. "Fine.
Everything's fine."

"Good. I'm glad." Concern faded and his eyes became guarded when he noticed Karina standing on
the concrete porch beside him. "Hello, Karina."

Her only answer was a stiff nod while she clutched
the purse strap hanging from her shoulder.

*Great. She's holding a grudge against my only
reliable contact in New Mexico. And Parker knows
it, too.*

Only to be expected, he supposed, since Parker
had arrested her brother. Karina was smarter than to
blame him for Alex's situation, though. She'd better
get over her antagonism soon, because Mason was
coming up short on people to ask for help in this mess.

"Can we come in?" he asked.

"Yeah, of course." Parker stepped back into the
house and gestured for them to enter.

Mason waited until Karina crossed the threshold,
then followed her inside. His glance circled a cav-
ernous but empty entry hall while Parker closed the
door behind them. A living room off to one side was
sparsely furnished with a battered but sturdy coffee
table and end tables, and the same worn sofa and
matching chair he remembered from Parker's apart-

ment years before. A set of carpeted stairs to the right led to the upper floor.

"Nice house," he commented. "You lived here long?"

"I bought it a couple of years ago. Decided it was time to make an investment instead of throwing my paycheck away on rent every month."

"Nice. Your decorating taste hasn't improved any since I saw you last, though." Mason accompanied the jab with a friendly grin.

Parker followed his glance to the living room, then laughed. "Yeah? Well, I don't spend much time in there. But take a look in here."

They followed him past the stairway to the place where the short entry hall opened into the main part of the house.

"Wow." Mason stopped and sent an admiring glace around. "Now *that's* what I'm talking about."

A great room ran the length of the house, with a kitchen on the left and a long den on the right. A big stone fireplace dominated the far wall, and a large flat-screen television hung suspended between two windows along the back. Plush leather recliners and a sofa were arranged around the television. Though devoid of decorating touches, the room had everything needed for a guy's haven, the perfect place to kick back on a Sunday afternoon and watch the big game.

"Yeah, that fireplace is why I bought the house." He rubbed his hands together and winked. "Let me tell you, man, it's popular with women on a cold winter night after a romantic dinner." The grin halted half-formed on his lips, then faded into chagrin when he caught sight of Karina's hard stare. "Uh, anyway. The house is great."

Same old Parker. He always was a ladies' man. Apparently he continued to enjoy female attentions while avoiding matrimonial entanglements, just like always.

"Anyway, grab a seat."

He dropped into one of the recliners, and Mason took the other. Karina, her demeanor silent and disapproving, perched on the edge of the thickly cushioned sofa, her knees together and her purse clutched in both hands in her lap. Her attitude was beginning to grate on his nerves.

"We just came from talking to Alex at juvy." Mason forced himself to relax against the soft leather.

Parker's expression settled into one of polite inquiry. "Yeah? How's he doing?"

Mason shrugged a shoulder. "As well as can be expected. Insists he didn't do anything wrong."

His friend responded with a snort. "Every caged bird sings that song."

On the sofa Karina's posture stiffened even further as she drew herself up. "He *didn't* do anything wrong."

Mason cast a warning glance in her direction, then spoke to Parker. "I know you can't tell me anything official because you're involved in the case, but anything you can give me off the record would be great. I've got nothing to go on."

He seemed to consider the request for a moment, then gave a slight nod. With a glance in the direction of the sofa, he angled his body slightly toward Mason. "Look, neither of these kids have been in any trouble before, but they both have a rep. There's been talk of gang affiliations for a few months now."

"That's a lie." Karina was on her feet in an instant. "Alex and José don't run with gangs. They aren't that kind of teenager."

Parker's impatience flared. "Yeah? What kind of teenager runs the streets of Albuquerque at two in the morning? And don't tell me you buy that lame story of going out for a harmless walk." His lips twisted. "I'm *sure* there are lots of harmless activities that go on in a dark alley at that hour."

If Mason thought he had a corner on the sarcasm market, he was wrong. Parker had him beat hands down, and his tone would slice through steel. It stopped Karina in her tracks.

Besides, he was right. Alex's story of taking a harmless walk in the middle of the night was clearly untrue. He'd seen it on the boy's face.

But Karina's crumpled expression reached down deep inside him and twisted. She sank slowly back to her seat looking suddenly small.

"Look," Mason told Parker, "we don't know what was going down, and Alex is clammed up tighter than a rusty lug nut. But whatever happened that night, I haven't seen anything to convince me he killed that kid."

Parker held up a finger. "The dead kid's blood on his hands and clothes." He extended additional fingers as he listed the evidence. "A stolen handgun on the ground beside him, which turned out to be the murder weapon. His prints all over it. No corroborating witnesses to the presence of a mugger. Pretty convincing if you ask me."

Karina spoke, but this time in a more subdued tone. "José died in his arms. That's how the blood got there."

The look Parker gave her bordered on pity.

"Actually the blood supports his claim, if you ask me," Mason said. "If he'd shot his friend, wouldn't he have taken off immediately? He wouldn't have stuck around long enough to get covered in blood."

Parker tilted his head, considering, and then conceded the point with a nod. "That makes sense."

"Besides, what's the motive? That's what I keep coming back to. These kids were friends."

"Yeah, but they're also teenagers with known gang affiliations." He shot a quick glance toward Karina and corrected himself. "*Suspected* gang affiliations. But gangsters or not, you know how hotheaded teenage boys are. They could have had an argument, lost their tempers, took things a little too far."

"No." Karina said it quietly, but with certainty. "Alex would never let an argument go far enough to lose control like that. He's my brother. I've been with him every day since he was born, and I know he would never hurt anyone no matter what."

Parker matched her volume and spoke with equal control. "I'm sure he's a great kid under normal circumstances. But drugs make people do terrible things that they would never do if they were straight."

Her jaw dropped, as though she were stunned momentarily speechless. Mason had wondered if drugs could have been a factor, but he'd been hesitant to ask Alex with his sister in the room.

"Did you find anything on him?" he asked.

Parker shook his head. "But I checked with the lab this morning. High levels of THC and trace amounts of methamphetamine in both of them."

Meth. Mason gave a low whistle. That stuff made people crazy. But if there were only traces of meth, then at least Alex wasn't messed up when the crime occurred. But the presence of any street drugs at all, especially meth, would look bad with the judge. And high levels of THC meant Alex had probably been smoking marijuana that night.

"I can't believe it." Unshed tears sparkled in Karina's shocked eyes. Her hands lay limply in her lap. "Alex is on drugs? It can't be true."

Parker answered in a gentle tone. "I'm sorry. Blood tests don't lie."

Something still didn't sound right. Mason leaned forward, arms resting on his knees, thinking out loud. "So he wasn't tweaking Friday night or there would have been more than a trace of meth in his blood."

He looked at his old partner. "Pot makes you mellow, not antagonistic. That sounds even less like José's death was the result of an argument gone bad. So I still can't see a motive."

Parker stared at him a moment, then shrugged. "I don't know, buddy. That's the D.A.'s job. I just do the legwork."

Which was exactly what Mason was there to do—legwork. Only he'd be searching for evidence to clear Alex of any wrongdoing, not to convict him. At least he had inside help from his old partner. It was almost like old times, working together to dig up evidence the district attorney could use to get a conviction on the criminals they'd arrested.

But the last case they worked together was different. That time they'd been looking for evidence to prove that he didn't kill his wife. And they'd nearly come up empty-handed.

His throat suddenly dry, he swallowed and asked, "Any ID on the weapon yet?"

"Haven't heard anything. I can check, though, and let you know."

"Thanks. Another thing. We seemed to have picked up a tail, a goon in a black Impala."

"Really?" Parker straightened, his forehead creasing. "Do you think this has anything to do with the case against the kid?"

Mason exchanged a glance with Karina. "Yeah. I do."

Parker blew out a breath in a long, steady stream. "You get a tag?"

"Not yet. But if he shows up again, I may need some help."

He found himself the object of a long, sober stare.

"If this is true—" Parker held up a hand to forestall an argument "— and I don't doubt you at all, then that puts a whole different slant on the case. If this guy shows up again, you'll call me, right?"

Mason allowed himself a grim smile. His old partner had lost none of his edge. Mason understood the implications immediately. If the guy watching Karina had anything to do with Alex, then that would almost guarantee that Alex was mixed up with some sort of gang. He glanced at Karina, who was watching him with questions in her eyes.

"You bet I will," he assured Parker.

"Hey, listen, do you need a place to stay?" Parker's gaze slid toward Karina, then turned back to Mason. A sly grin twisted his lips. "I mean, unless you two are..." He waggled his eyebrows.

"No, we're not," Karina said loudly at the same time Mason said, "It's not like that."

Parker's eyes rounded, while Mason avoided looking toward the sofa. An awkward silence descended on the room. So far he and Karina had avoided discussing their previous relationship, and Mason preferred to keep it that way. Though he had loved Karina once, a chasm stretched between that time and now, a ravine filled with guilt and painful words and unforgiven injuries. He couldn't imagine opening himself up to love another woman again. Margie was still so much a part of his life, still very much alive in his memories. But if he did ever manage to have romantic feelings for another woman, it wouldn't be Karina. Margie's presence was one of those ghosts Caleb was referring to, and she would always hover between them.

"So anyway." Parker's voice cut through the silence. "If you need a place to stay while you're in town, I've got a couple of spare rooms upstairs. There's even a bed in one of them, and you're welcome to it. But not until tomorrow. Today's my day off, and I'm having a party tonight." He leaned sideways across the arm of his chair toward Mason and winked. "A private party."

On the couch Karina emitted a grunt of disgust and rolled her eyes expansively.

Mason ignored her. "Thanks. I might take you up on that." Not only would it save a couple of bucks, if he and Parker could spend a few hours alone talking about the case without Karina around, they might come up with something helpful.

They spent a few minutes catching up on old friends Mason had forgotten existed. Talking to Parker was like opening the pages of an old photo album. Faces rose in his mind like ancient photographs. Old cases they worked together. Incidents recorded in distant memory replayed, most of them good. He'd almost forgotten that he did have a life in Albuquerque apart from Margie. Apart from Karina.

Long before he was finished with his stroll down memory lane, Karina's patience evaporated. She stood abruptly and shouldered her purse.

"We need to go." The statement was more than a demand.

"Uh, yeah. I guess we'll leave you to get ready for your date." Mason got to his feet and held out his hand toward Parker. "I'll give you a call tomorrow."

"Sounds good." When Parker released his hand, they headed toward the door, Karina in the lead. "Do me one favor, would you?"

"Of course." Mason turned at the front to face his friend. "Name it."

Parker's gaze dropped away. "If you happen to run into Detective Grierson, don't say anything about me helping you."

Grierson. The mention of the familiar name hit Mason like a slab of concrete from the sky. From the moment he'd agreed to come to Albuquerque yesterday, that was one person he had avoided thinking of, even though the name of his former sergeant dangled at the edges of his mind like a hand grenade without a pin, waiting to explode.

So Sergeant Grierson was now Detective Grierson. A different rank than the one he'd held as Mason's boss, with weightier responsibilities. If Grierson had possessed the power of a detective four years ago, Mason would no doubt be in prison right now.

"No fears about that," Mason assured him. "I'm going to do everything I can not to run into Grierson."

"Probably a good idea."

On the way to the driveway Mason studied the street in both directions. No sign of the Impala, or any other suspicious-looking vehicles. The fact didn't make him feel much better, though. The absence of a watching goon didn't mean there wasn't one there. It might mean they'd decided to change their observation tactics to stealth mode. And that they were good at it.

SIX

Karina seated herself and slammed the car door closed. "Alex is not on drugs," she told Mason with a glare that dared him to disagree. "I would have seen some sign."

Mason snapped his seat belt without looking at her. "Some kids who use drugs get to be pretty good at covering their tracks. Alex has always been a smart kid. Parents, or guardians in your case, are often the last to know."

Fury roiled up inside her, so huge that she almost couldn't breathe. How dare he come here after four years and assume he knew *anything* about Alex? Or about her, for that matter?

She tightened her grip on the steering wheel and forced air into her lungs. A familiar buzz filled her head, a sign of elevated blood pressure. If she didn't calm down soon, she'd end up having a stroke like the one that killed her father.

Mason wasn't the bad guy here. She needed to keep reminding herself of that, and stop letting her anger over the past affect her ability to deal with him now. He'd come at her request, and he wanted to help Alex.

Lord, I'm not handling this situation well. Please help me to stay calm. And if there is something about Alex I need to know, please help me to see the truth.

There. She felt the blood pressure buzz begin to recede as she drew in deep, slow breaths. Prayer was the best thing she could do, for herself and for Alex. Sometimes she forgot that.

"I understand that," she admitted. Mason looked up at her, his expression skeptical. "Really. But you don't know Alex like I do. I'm not just his guardian, I'm his sister. He tells me everything, especially since Papa died."

"Blood tests don't lie." His words, spoken in a soft, compassionate voice, cut deeper than a razor blade.

"Maybe there was a mistake at the lab," she shot back. "They could have gotten Alex's blood mixed up with someone else's."

His compassion turned to pity, and showed on his face. Tears threatened, and she blinked furiously to control them as she turned the key to start the car. She was grasping at straws, and they both knew it. She put the car in Reverse and zoomed out of the driveway.

"Where are we going?" Mason asked as she sped away from Parker Harding's house.

"To talk to José's mother. I have to know if she suspected José of being on drugs."

What Karina really meant was she had to know

if she really was as clueless about Alex's activities as it was starting to look. But she saw no reason to admit that to Mason.

The Garcias lived in a small, cracker-box-shaped house in a neighborhood a few blocks from Karina's apartment. She'd been there a couple of times to pick up José and chauffeur the boys to the movie theater, or to a church youth group event.

The homes that lined the block weren't nearly as nice as those in Parker Harding's neighborhood. No grass grew in the yards, though a few sported enough dust-colored weeds to resemble a lawn. Rusty cars lined the curb. Karina followed a school bus down the street and watched as the bus disgorged dozens of mostly Hispanic children who walked away in small clusters. She parked the car at the curb in front of the Garcias' house and cut the engine. Silence settled in the interior of the car as they both inspected the door and the closed blinds at the windows. For some reason the house looked forlorn and sad. School children stared through the windshield as they walked past on the sidewalk.

"José has several brothers and sisters," Karina said, watching the kids walk by the house. "I guess they aren't going to school this week."

"When's the funeral?" Mason's voice was quiet, subdued, as he stared at the front door.

"Tomorrow." The knots in Karina's stomach tightened and churned. Her memories of Mama's funeral when Alex was a baby were vague, fogged over by the pain of loss. Papa's funeral was fresher, having occurred just last year. That was horribly sad, of course, but how much sadder would a funeral for a fourteen-year-old boy be?

Her nerves danced with anxious thoughts. How would Mr. and Mrs. Garcia receive them? If they believed the police report and the terrible accusations reported in the newspaper and on television the past few days, they might not be happy about a visit from the sister of the boy accused of murdering their son.

I have to convince them that Alex didn't do it.

Her determination settled, she took the keys from the ignition. "Are you ready?"

"Might as well get it over with." Mason's tight-lipped expression told her he felt just as anxious as she did. For some reason that made her feel a tiny bit better.

They exited the car. Karina fidgeted with a lock of unruly hair as she crossed the yard. What would she say to Mrs. Garcia? There were no words, English or Spanish, to express the depth of her sympathy.

The front door opened before they'd approached the small concrete square that served as a porch. A Hispanic woman flew out, and in the next minute Karina found herself caught up in a smothering embrace, Mrs. Garcia's sobs filling her ears.

"No lo creó," she muttered over and over. *"Alex no haría esta cosa."* I don't believe it. Alex would not do this thing.

Relief welled up from deep within Karina as Mrs. Garcia's words fell on her ears. *She doesn't believe the lies!* She held the woman and sobbed with relief and in shared grief.

"Gracias." She repeated multiple times as their grief found mutual release. *"Gracias."*

She gradually became aware that a man stood in the doorway watching them. Short and lean, his narrow face was drawn and haggard. José's father. His expression held the same deep grief as his wife's, his eyes red with unshed tears. Standing beside her, Mason shuffled his feet in the dirt and weeds, his hands shoved in the pockets of his jeans, his gaze wandering up and down the street.

Mrs. Garcia pulled back, though she did not release Karina's arm. "Come inside. Have a cold drink. We talk, you and I."

Karina turned an unspoken command toward Mason to follow her as she was pulled forward and through the front door. Mr. Garcia stepped back to let them enter, then closed the door behind them, his movements slow and heavy.

She looked at the man as she performed the introductions. "Mr. and Mrs. Garcia, this is my friend, Mason Sinclair. He flew here from Atlanta this morning to try to help me figure out what really happened the night José was—" a hard swallow "—killed."

Mr. Garcia maintained his silence while he shook Mason's hand. Then José's mother released Karina to pull Mason into a tight embrace. She collapsed

over his shoulder, crying over and over, *"¡Mi hijo!"*
My son!

Mason tossed a startled glance toward Karina,
and then patted the woman's back awkwardly as she
cried.

After a moment she pulled away. *"Lo siento.* I am
sorry to cry on you, *señor."*

"Uh, no problem." He glanced at José's father and
ducked his head. "I'm very sorry for your loss."

A trio of faces appeared at the doorway as Mrs.
Garcia invited them to be seated on the couch. José's
brothers and sister. Karina smiled in their direction.
The little girl, probably around four, giggled and disappeared down the hallway at a run. The two boys
followed more slowly, their expressions solemn.

"Alex is a good boy, a good friend to José," Mrs.
Garcia told Karina as soon as they were seated. "I
tell the *policía*, but they arrest him anyway."

"Thank you for doing that." Karina glanced at
Mason, who sat there with his lips a tight, silent line.
It looked like the talking would be up to her this
time. "Mrs. Garcia, do you know what happened that
night? When did the boys leave the house?"

The woman shook her head. "I did not hear them
leave. They were watching the television. We go to
bed around ten o'clock." She glanced at her husband
for confirmation, and he nodded. "The police wake
us up at three to tell us our José is dead. Shot with a
gun." Fresh tears filled her eyes.

So they hadn't heard the boys leave the house. She

hesitated before asking the next question. What if they hadn't been told the results of the lab report yet? She didn't want to be the one to tell them that their son had drugs in his system.

"Have you noticed any changes in José lately? Anything at all?"

Both parents nodded without hesitation.

"He has money now. He gives us money for the food, and the…" She waved her hand toward the lamp, searching for a word. "The electric. And he buy clothes and toys for the little ones."

Mason had apparently decided to break his silence. "Did you ask him how he came by the money?"

"He get a job, work after school and every Saturday." Mr. Garcia spoke for the first time, his voice a high tenor, his accent even more prominent than his wife's. "A good boy, my José. A hard worker."

Mason leaned forward and rested his arms on his thighs. "Where did he work?"

"Casa del Sol Restaurante. He clean the tables, wash the dishes, sweep the floor, whatever they want him to do. He never complain."

"Do you mind telling me how much money he gave you?"

Karina narrowed her eyes. Where was he going with that question?

"Three hundred dollars every month." The man straightened in his chair, his chest swelling with pride. "Is makes more than me."

Three hundred dollars? Karina was impressed.

Alex had also gotten a job at the beginning of the summer, bagging groceries and stocking shelves at a small grocery store in the neighborhood. He had also given her money to help with the bills, about thirty dollars a week. Karina had felt guilty taking that, because it was more than half of his take-home pay.

"Hmm." Mason nodded. "Any other changes? Was he moodier than normal the last few months? Depressed, maybe?"

Both shook their heads.

Mason pushed. "Or overly energetic?"

Karina gave him a cautious look. The Garcias needed to hear about the blood test from the police, not from them.

Again they shook their heads.

"And no fights with Alex," Mrs. Garcia added. She looked at Karina. "The *policía* ask, and we tell them. Alex is like a brother to José."

Before Karina could thank her, the doorbell chimed. Mrs. Garcia leaped up from her chair and rushed to answer. Another woman stood on the front stoop, a big covered bowl in her hands and a mournful expression on her face.

"Apesadumbrado para su pérdida." I'm sorry for your loss.

At the woman's expression of sympathy, José's mother once again dissolved into tears. The grief offering was passed off to Mr. Garcia while the two women embraced, their tears mingled. The spicy aroma of cooked onions and peppers filled the small room.

Karina caught Mason's eye. It was time to leave. She'd accomplished what she wanted from the visit, to express her deep sympathy and to make sure the Garcias didn't blame Alex for their son's death. Mason nodded, and they stood.

"Thank you for talking with us," Karina told Mr. Garcia. She gave the woman a final hug, and said, "You will be in my prayers."

"Gracias," she muttered before returning to her new visitor. "And Alex will be in mine."

Karina left the house, Mason close on her heels. Neither of them spoke until they were in the car and heading down the road.

"Remind me never to do that again. My shirt is soaked from all those tears." His voice snapped with irritation.

She glanced sideways at him, angered by his tone. A sharp retort died on her lips when she caught sight of his strained expression. No doubt he'd found the visit upsetting. The Garcias' grief probably stirred up memories of his own loss.

He hasn't gotten over his wife's death.

The thought brought none of the anger she occasionally still felt when she thought of Mason's wife. Instead compassion stirred within her. He must have loved her very much to still feel her loss so keenly after four years. How hard these past years must have been for him.

She schooled her voice. "Well, at least we know the Garcias don't think Alex shot their son."

She pressed on the gas pedal, and the car responded sluggishly. *Oh no. I hope it's not getting ready to die again. I can't afford a big car repair bill.*

"Not only that," Mason replied, "but we found out something even more important. José had a lot of money recently."

She glanced at him and pumped the gas pedal to keep the engine from dying. "Of course he did. He got a job at the beginning of the summer, just like Alex."

"Oh, come on. You don't think he made three hundred dollars a month working after school and on Saturdays, do you? Plus they said he was buying clothes and stuff for the younger kids on top of that. Minimum wage for students in New Mexico is $6.38 an hour. Even if his boss was paying him regular minimum wage, which is $7.50, you have to figure in taxes and social security and all that stuff. He would have had to be putting in a lot of hours."

It was true. Karina saw that immediately. Alex didn't bring home nearly that much, and she didn't think José had worked any more hours than Alex.

"So if he didn't get the money from his job, where did he get it?" She hated to ask the question, because she already knew Mason's answer before he said it.

"He could have been selling drugs." He glanced sideways at her. "Which might mean Alex was involved too."

Even though she'd anticipated his answer, she shook her head. "No. I don't believe it."

The car's forward speed slowed, and she pumped the gas pedal. *No! I can't afford to have car trouble.*

Mason sniffed. "Do you smell gasoline?"

The moment he said the words she realized she'd smelled gas since she'd started the engine.

"I think I'm having car trouble," she told him. "The engine keeps trying to die."

"Pull over." He pointed to an empty place along the curb. "Pop the hood and let me take a look."

She did as he requested. He put on his sunglasses, got out of the car, and disappeared from view when he raised the hood.

"Give some gas," his voice shouted.

Karina did.

In the next instant an explosion shook the car. At the same instant, she saw his body thrown sideways, into the street.

"Mason!"

SEVEN

Mason sat on the edge of a stretcher. His shirt lay in shreds on the pavement, compliments of the EMT who stood in front of him swabbing at his shoulder with a moist sterile pad. A crowd gathered on the sidewalk across the street to gawk, drawn by the flashing red lights of the emergency workers. A couple of police officers had asked a few preliminary questions, and were now inspecting the damage to the car's engine along with the firemen. At least the fire was out, though it had probably rendered Karina's car a total loss.

It had almost done the same to him.

The EMT's pad scraped across his abused skin and Mason couldn't hold back a hiss. The pain from the burns hurt more than he wanted to admit.

The young man immediately pulled back. "Sorry. There's some dirt in that one. I'm going to leave it alone and let the Emergency Room folks handle it."

"No, go ahead and clean me up, then slap a bandage or something on it. I'm not going to the hospital," Mason said for the third time.

"Yes, you are." Karina stood directly in front of him, hands on her hips, glaring like a drill sergeant. "Those burns are going to get infected if they're not treated properly." Her eyes moved as her gaze swept his face. "And they'll scar, too. You don't want that, do you?"

When she called attention to his face, he became more aware of the burning pain there, as well. He'd lost some hair on the left side of his head, his ear stung like crazy and he probably wouldn't be able to shave for a while, judging by the burning on his left cheekbone. Thank goodness he'd been wearing sunglasses, or his injuries might have been more severe.

He gave her a rakish grin, ignoring the pain the movement caused his damaged skin. "A scar will make me look like a pirate who's been in a sword fight, don't you think?"

She didn't return the smile. "No, I don't. Burn scars aren't the same as sword scars. Your skin will get all puckered and you'll look like a lizard."

A lizard? He killed the grin. Maybe he'd run along to the hospital after all, just to let them check it out. Judging by the sharp pain every time he took a deep breath, he might have cracked a rib when he hit the pavement, but he wasn't about to let on to Karina about that.

Another siren sounded, and a white Charger with blue lights flashing from the front grill pulled up behind the fire truck. Ah, the investigating detective must have arrived. Wouldn't it be an amazing coincidence if the detective turned out to be—

Mason stiffened, and the movement sent pain through the damaged, burned skin of his shoulder and chest. The man who emerged from the driver's seat of the Dodge was none other than Curt Grierson, his former police sergeant.

Standing beside his car, Grierson scanned the area and his gaze came to rest on Mason. Recognition dawned, but not surprise, which meant he'd already been given their names. He slammed his car door and crossed the distance between them with long, purposeful strides.

"When you decide to make a comeback you don't waste time, do you, Sinclair?"

Mason forced himself to control his features, though inside he seethed with indignation. No greeting. No *How've you been?* from his former boss, not that he'd expected a friendly reception. Four years ago Grierson had made no secret of the fact that he thought Mason was on the take, and that his illegal activities were somehow responsible for Margie's death.

"Well you know me, Sergeant," he responded with forced ease, "I never could keep a low profile."

"It's detective." Grierson's lips tightened beneath his moustache. "Has been for four years now. Since shortly after you left, in fact."

What was that supposed to mean? That getting rid of Mason had been good for his career? The jerk was baiting him. Mason dropped all semblance of politeness. "Congratulations on the promotion. Since I wasn't available, who'd you have to frame to get that?"

The EMT packed up his gear and made a quick escape toward the back of the ambulance. Beside him Karina's expression froze.

Mason halfway hoped Grierson would rise to the insult. Being nearly blown up left him in a bad mood, and a verbal argument with the guy who had treated him like a criminal during the worst episode of his life might be just the thing. Instead Grierson actually smiled. The expression looked foreign on his stern lips.

"Still the same smart aleck tongue, I see. What are you doing in town, Sinclair?"

"Visiting some old friends." He sent a warning glance to Karina. No sense telling this guy anything if they didn't have to.

"Looks like some of them aren't too happy to see you." Grierson's glanced slid pointedly to the car. The blackened residue of the fire could still be seen on the raised hood from this distance.

"Oh, just a little engine trouble."

"It was not!" Karina glared in his direction and took a step toward the detective. "My car was blown up, Detective, and Mason could have been killed."

Great. Now she'd stirred up a hornet's nest. Mason returned her glare with disgust. She never could keep her mouth shut when she should.

"Blown up? As in, with an explosive device?" Grierson's eyebrows rose.

Mason didn't bother to hold back a sigh. Being evasive with this guy, jerk or not, wouldn't do any good. He'd get all the information he needed from the police reports anyway. And Mason wasn't stupid enough to hold back on a police report. Especially when Karina's safety might be at jeopardy.

"Not a device. Somebody cut a hole in the gas line right next to the catalytic converter, which was hot from our driving around town. The harder we stomped on the pedal, the more gas squirted directly onto it. I happened to be looking under the hood when the gasoline ignited." Mason's head went a little light at the memory. If he hadn't seen what was happening and jerked backward at the right moment, his injuries would have been much more severe. A close call, much too close for his liking.

"What do you mean *somebody poked a hole?*" The detective's eyes narrowed. "Sounds like a faulty fuel line to me."

"My car was not having any mechanical problems." Karina folded her arms. "It was the man who's been following me. It must be."

Grierson's head jerked around to give Mason a hard stare. "I think you'd better start at the beginning, Sinclair."

Mason did, succinctly and with clipped words. "Karina noticed a man in a black car parked outside her apartment yesterday, watching her. Today she and

I visited her brother in juvy and when we came out we found the same guy in the parking lot, surveilling her car. Big guy, arms like a wrestler. He drove off before I could get his plates. The car drove fine when we left there." He glanced at Karina for verification, and she nodded. No need to mention the visit to Parker's house. "Then just now we were paying a visit to a house a couple of streets over. Couldn't have been inside more than ten minutes. Long enough for someone to mess with the gas line, if they knew what they were doing."

Though Grierson's expression had not changed when Mason mentioned juvy, he pounced on that detail, as Mason had known he would.

"Who's the brother, and why's he there?"

"His name is Alexander Guerrero."

Recognition dawned on the detective's face. He folded his arms and stood in front of Mason with his feet spaced at shoulder's length. "The kid who killed his friend this weekend."

Karina's hot reply was instant. "He did not."

Mason allowed a cold smile as he returned Grierson's stare. "Innocent until proven guilty, remember, Sergeant?"

Grierson ignored the title jab. "All right. *Suspected* of killing another kid in a gang-style shooting. I'm familiar with the case, since my team handled the arrest. Or did you know that already?"

A prod for information, but one Mason wasn't going to fall for. No way would he say anything to get Parker in hot water. Instead he fired back a snappy reply. "Really? You handled the arrest? You've expanded your area of expertise from innocent patrol officers to innocent teenagers, then?"

"One of my officers did." His eyes narrowed. "Your old partner, Harding."

Mason worked hard to keep his face impassive, and he thought he succeeded. After a long silence during which they engaged in a staring contest, Grierson cocked his head sideways, his gaze shrewd.

"You know what I find interesting, Sinclair? You pop up after several years, and suddenly we have another gang-style shooting on our hands. Don't you find that interesting?"

A sudden and nearly irresistible anger flared, clouding any snappy reply Mason could have made. His hands tightened at his sides. He'd been completely cleared of all charges in Margie's death, but Grierson still treated him like a suspect.

Karina thrust herself between them, fury evident in the corded muscles in her slender neck. "That's ridiculous. Mason didn't get here until today. The only reason he came is because I asked him for help. I knew if my brother's fate was left up to people like *you*," she spat the word, "who rush to believe he's guilty without giving him a chance, he'll be convicted of a crime he didn't commit."

The force of Karina's fury dampened Mason's. Several strands of thick hair had come loose from their binding, and stood out around her head. She looked like a feral cat, back arched, fur standing at attention and spitting mad.

But of course she'd just let a piece of information slip. Grierson picked up on it immediately. He looked at Mason over Karina's head.

"You're here to investigate?"

Mason didn't answer. The less this guy knew about his activities, the better.

Grim faced, the detective raised a hand and pointed a finger in his direction. "I'm going to say this once. You stay out of this investigation. If I hear your name come up even once in relation to this case, I'll arrest you for obstruction. Do you understand?"

Several responses came to mind, but Mason clamped his jaw shut on them. He wasn't licensed in New Mexico, so while there was nothing to prevent him from asking questions, he didn't have the protection of a P.I. license to back him up. Grierson could do exactly as he threatened.

He jerked a nod in acknowledgment of the warning. "But what about the tail she's picked up? She might need police protection."

Not that he wanted an officer following them around and reporting their activities back to Grierson. But if that goon came back to finish the job, he might not be able to protect Karina alone. Especially since he wasn't allowed to carry a weapon in this state.

The detective's mouth pursed. "If it turns out to

be something other than a faulty fuel line, we'll talk about it."

With that he turned on a heel and stomped toward the car and the officers standing near it.

Mason glanced at Karina and a protective instinct flamed in him, almost akin to the passion he'd once felt. She'd let her guard down and for a moment looked so scared and alone, he vowed to take care of her. Her expression steeled as she turned to face him, and Mason checked his emotions. Karina wanted his help, but she'd never accept his protection or his passion. It was far too late for that.

EIGHT

The Emergency Room doors whooshed open, and Karina slipped a hand inside Mason's arm to help him outside. The poor guy looked like a mummy, with bandages wrapped around his head, his shoulder and a wide one around his ribs beneath the spare shirt he'd donned from his overnight bag. His injuries were her fault, and she felt terrible for getting him into this mess. At least the hospital doctor didn't seem concerned. She had loaded them up with ointment and instructions to keep the burned areas clean, and to drink plenty of fluid to replace lost electrolytes.

Mason jerked his arm away, then sucked in his breath in a hiss, his hand going to his injured and wrapped ribs. "I'm not an invalid," he snapped.

"Of course you're not." Karina kept her face impassive. Pain always had put him in a bad mood. He'd refused the doctor's offer of pain medication, though. Stubborn as ever.

They moved toward the taxicab waiting for them at the end of the wheelchair ramp. She rushed a few steps ahead and opened the door for him, which earned her a glare.

"Don't coddle me." His voice held an ill-tempered warning as he ducked into the backseat. "I don't need any help."

She bit back a sigh, and adjusted the strap of his overnight bag on her shoulder as she slid in beside him. The only thing more irritating than the sarcastic Mason was the in-pain-and-trying-not-to-show-it Mason.

When they'd given the cab driver directions to take them to the rental car place, she sat back and watched the Albuquerque streets through the window. All the things she needed to do flitted through her mind. A call to the insurance company topped the list. She carried full coverage, required since she'd borrowed money to buy the car, but how would they handle it when she owed more than the car was worth? Thank goodness Mason had offered to rent a car for the few days he would be in town. When he left, she wasn't sure what she'd do for transportation.

But the problem of a car seemed insignificant when she thought of how close they'd come to being blown up.

She glanced sideways at Mason, and spoke in a low voice so the cab driver couldn't hear. "I can't believe someone tried to kill us."

"They weren't trying to kill us." He fidgeted with the bandage on his left arm. "If they'd wanted us dead, there are a dozen other ways they could have rigged that car. That was a warning. They're letting us know they're watching."

The seriousness of their situation washed over her again. "Who are they, Mason? What is Alex mixed up in?"

"I don't know." He held her gaze. "You realize that all this points toward gang activity, don't you?"

She looked down at her hands in her lap. How could Alex be involved in gangs, and using drugs? Surely there had been signs. How could she have missed them? Guilt flooded her in a warm wave. Alex was her responsibility, and she'd failed him.

"Yes," she answered in a whisper. "I know."

"Hey." The voice he used was tender, the one she sometimes remembered from happier days. He covered her cold hands with a warm one, and something stirred deep inside her. "He's a good kid. He always was. Kids these days have a harder time than we did. Everything is so available to them. Drugs. Alcohol. They all experiment. Maybe this will be a wake-up call for him."

Tears blurred her vision as she stared at his strong hand covering hers. "You don't think he killed José, do you, Mason?"

"No." The certainty in his tone strengthened her own faith in her brother. Someone else believed in his innocence, too. "I don't know what's happening, but I'm positive Alex didn't kill anybody." His hand squeezed hers. "We're going to get to the bottom of this, Karina."

Gratitude swelled her throat, and she couldn't speak. She blinked away tears and smiled her thanks.

Mason removed his hand, and his voice returned to normal. "So I've been thinking about our next move. If Grierson hadn't showed up, I would have stuck around to question the witnesses, see if anyone noticed someone monkeying around with your car while we were inside the Garcias'. Maybe Parker can find out something for us tomorrow."

The taxi slowed and pulled into the car rental company's parking lot. A short line of customers waited at the counter inside a glass-front building.

"What do we do now?"

Mason winced with pain as he shifted in his seat to pull his billfold out of his back pocket. "It's time for supper, isn't it?"

Karina glanced at her watch. Almost seven. The hospital visit had taken a couple of hours. "Yes, but I don't think I can eat." She'd barely been able to choke down anything since Alex was arrested Friday night.

"Well, I can. Being blown up makes me hungry."

The grin he turned on her was the old Mason, the one she used to love.

The old passion stirred, trying to resurface from deep inside, to rise out of the ashes of hurt and anger that had smothered them. A sudden longing filled her. Oh, if only they could wipe away the past four years and return to those days, those feelings. Once, she had given her heart to him, and when he grinned like that, she wanted desperately to believe they could recover what they'd lost. But how could she open herself to him again? What if he hurt her a second time? She feared she wouldn't survive.

Unaware of the turmoil that raged inside her, Mason counted out the cab fare. "Besides, I think we need to pay a visit to Casa del Sol Restaurante."

Karina forced herself to return his grin. "The restaurant where José worked."

"Exactly." He handed the money to the cab driver in the front seat, and tucked the receipt into his billfold. "Grierson warned us off poking around, but he can't fault us for going out to dinner, can he?"

The restaurant was located in one end of a strip mall a mile or so from the Garcias' neighborhood. Mason parked the rental car in the parking lot out front and studied the building. Windows on either side of the door were darkened with blinds on the inside, and decorated with signs. Glowing blue and red neon advertised beer for sale, beside a poster of an upcoming street festival and a handmade flyer in Spanish advertising puppies for sale. The day's special, enchiladas in red sauce with rice and beans for $6.99, was printed on a chalkboard hanging to the right of the door.

"This doesn't look like a place that can afford to pay a busboy much," he commented to Karina.

"No, it doesn't." She waved a hand to indicate the small number of cars in the parking lot. "They don't seem to be very busy, either."

Mason didn't verbalize the obvious conclusion, that José must have gotten his money from somewhere other than his job at the restaurant. No sense rubbing it in. Karina wasn't stupid. She knew what that meant. If José was selling drugs, then Alex was probably involved as well.

She turned in the passenger seat to look at him, her eyes sweeping over his face. "I wish you'd leave the bandage on like the doctor said."

"Do you know how much attention I'll draw if I walk around with a bandage wrapped around my head?"

"You're going to draw attention with half your hair burned off."

Mason glanced into the rearview mirror. The burns were confined to the left side of his head and his ear, and had singed a good portion of his hair. He'd been in the act of jerking away when the gasoline ignited on the hot catalytic converter. If he hadn't seen the gas squirt out a second before it sparked, he would have taken the brunt of the explosion in his face.

"Maybe I ought to just shave the whole thing. Then at least it'll be even."

She lifted a hand and ran her fingers through the hair on the right side of his head, as though testing its texture. It was a familiar touch, and sent a tingle through his scalp. A smile curved her lips for a moment, then she pulled her hand back and looked away.

"I think I can fix it without going to that extreme,

as long as you don't mind looking like you just joined the army."

The tingle faded, but left a disturbing sensation in Mason's stomach. For a moment they were the old Karina and Mason. When she was in cosmetology school she'd practiced on him until he had almost no hair left. But that was a lifetime ago, before he betrayed her with another woman.

"Or maybe the police academy."

The words, intended to break the weighted silence in the car, came out louder than he intended. She smiled again, but this time it faded quickly. He took the keys from the ignition and stuck a finger through the ring, jiggling them with a nervous gesture.

"Let's go see what this restaurant is like. I'm starving."

"All right."

She leaned over to pick up her purse, and at that moment the restaurant door opened. A pair of men stepped outside and stopped on the front sidewalk.

Mason froze with his hand on the door handle. The taller of the two looked familiar. He leaned forward and peered through the windshield. More gray lightened the dark hair, but the hawk nose and squared chin were the same. What were the odds of running into Maddox *and* Grierson on his first day back in Albuquerque? This man had haunted his thoughts in the months after Margie's death, before he'd learned to tame those thoughts and tuck them into the recesses of his mind where they couldn't bother him.

A fierce, hungry anger stirred up from the depths of his soul as the man put a toothpick in his mouth and shook hands in farewell to his companion. When he turned away, Mason got a look at his face full-on.

Yes, it was him. Russell Maddox, the owner of the fitness center where Margie had worked when she was murdered. The man Mason knew was somehow responsible for her death.

NINE

"Was that really Russell Maddox?"

The way Karina asked the question, with an almost breathless excitement that bordered on celebrity worship, set Mason's teeth on edge.

"Why do you ask it like that?" He snapped the question and pulled his water glass toward him with such an abrupt gesture that liquid sloshed over the edge and onto the scratched wooden tabletop.

"Because he's like a celebrity. People say he owns half of Albuquerque." A lock of dark hair swept the table when she leaned forward and lowered her voice. "He's one of the richest men in the whole state."

"So he's rich. So what?" He snatched the slice of lemon from the rim of his glass and squeezed with enough force that a torrent of juice splashed into the water. "I've never known you to be overly impressed with money."

"I'm not." She straightened and glanced around the restaurant. "But I never thought I'd see him in a regular restaurant. I figured he'd eat in swanky places. You know, the kind with big prices and tiny portions. Fifty dollars for three shrimp and a couple of asparagus spears."

"For cryin' out loud, he's just a guy. Maybe the food here's good, didja ever think of that?"

Her eyes narrowed, but instead of answering she raised her menu and hid behind the laminated page. He picked up his own menu and scanned the prices. Reasonable, cheap even. And a decent selection of typical Mexican dishes. Ten minutes ago he'd been starving, but the sight of Maddox had soured his stomach. What were the odds of running into him within minutes of Grierson? This day was turning into the nightmare of all reunions. He spared a nasty thought for Caleb. If his buddy had only kept his stupid mouth shut, Mason would be home in Atlanta right now.

For a year or two after he'd moved to Georgia, Mason's thoughts had hovered around Maddox almost to the point of obsession. His presence at Margie's funeral had caused a stir, the immaculate charcoal gray suit, dark maroon tie, perfectly coiffed hair and especially the carefully composed expression of sympathy. One of the television news shows made a point of showing a shot panning from Mason's grief-torn figure to Maddox's composed but carefully sorrowful one. "Russell Maddox, the grieving owner of Powerhouse Fitness, where newly employed aerobics instructor Marjorie Sinclair was brutally murdered, attended the victim's funeral on Saturday. Sinclair's husband, Albuquerque police officer Mason Sinclair, has been named as a person of interest in the investigation. No charges have yet been filed." All he had to do was close his eyes and he could still see that news report.

When the unbelievable occurred and Mason had been put on administrative leave while he was investigated for his own wife's murder, he'd gone into full investigation mode on his own. And everywhere he'd turned, one name kept cropping up. Russell Maddox. Parker, his old partner, had said it was just coincidence because the guy seemed to own half the city. But even though Mason's gut instinct had told him the guy was up to no good, he'd never uncovered a shred of evidence to prove it, and that had left a bad taste in his mouth that hadn't cleared in the past four years.

The waiter approached, a dark-skinned kid with straight black hair and Hispanic features. He set a bowl of tortilla chips and a dish of runny salsa on the table between them.

"What can I get you to drink?" Not a trace of accent sounded in his voice.

"I'm sticking with water," Mason replied.

"Something diet, please." Karina's gaze rose from her menu. "Was that really Russell Maddox we saw leaving a minute ago?"

His bored expression barely changed. "Yeah. He comes here a lot."

"Really?"

The kid nodded. "I guess he likes the enchiladas."

She grinned. "I'll bet he leaves a decent-size tip, huh?"

A shrug and an eye roll. "I never get to wait on him. He and the manager are friends or something. Jorge always takes care of Mr. Maddox personally."

He wandered off to get their drinks, and Mason leveled a disgusted glare across the table.

She returned the look calmly. "Wipe the glare off your face. I'm not impressed with his money. For your information, I have a reason for asking." She unwrapped the blue paper slip securing her napkin around her utensils.

She's going to make me ask. For some reason, that irritated him.

"So? Are you going to tell me?" he snapped.

Only when her napkin was smoothed in her lap did she answer. "Several times Alex mentioned seeing Russell Maddox in the store where he works. At the time I thought it was strange that a rich guy like him would shop in a dinky little grocery store like that, but I didn't give it much thought. But now." Her head moved as she looked around the room.

Mason followed her glance. On the inside this place was everything the outside had promised. Clean, but tiny and about as plain as you could get. Eight scarred wooden tables with hard plastic chairs. Fake tile floor scraped by the chair legs. Few attempts at decorations adorned the walls, mostly brightly colored ponchos and a display of cheap straw hats. Certainly nothing to attract the attention of a rich guy like Maddox. And apparently he ate here on a fairly regular basis.

A kind of sick excitement tickled the base of Mason's skull. "Those must be some killer enchiladas."

The look Karina gave him was full of understanding. "I can hardly wait to try them."

Maybe they'd stumbled onto something. If he could pin something on Maddox—anything, even a misdemeanor—that would make this trip worthwhile in Mason's books. His appetite stirred back to life.

The waiter returned and set Karina's soda on the table in front of her. "So do you know what you want?"

"Enchiladas, definitely," Mason said, and Karina nodded agreement. As the kid turned to leave, Mason stopped him with a word. "Hey, let me ask you a question. Did you work much with José Garcia?"

Finally, a reaction on the bored face. The smooth forehead creased, and his eyes darkened with grief. "Yeah. He was a buddy of mine."

"Terrible what happened to him." Mason shook his head in sympathy. "Getting shot by his friend and all."

Karina stiffened in her chair, and her mouth opened like she was getting ready to launch a verbal torpedo. He kept his gaze fixed on the server's face and kicked her under the table.

The teen's reaction almost mirrored Karina's. He seemed to grow a couple of inches taller as his spine stiffened. "They got no proof of that."

Mason picked up a straw and peeled the paper off. "The television folks seem pretty convinced."

The kid's expression became almost hostile. "I don't care what the TV says, mister, I don't believe it. I know Alex, too, a little, and there's no way he'd shoot José."

A smile spread across Karina's face, and her grateful eyes practically embraced the kid. Mason ignored her.

"Oh?" He shoved the straw into his glass and wadded the paper into a tight wad. "Were you there that night? Did you see what happened?"

His gaze fell away, and his weight shifted from one foot to the other. "No," he admitted.

"So if you didn't see what happened, then how do you know José's friend didn't shoot him, just like the police say he did?"

"I just know, that's all."

Mason pushed. "But how do you know?"

The kid didn't answer. His jaw became hard, stubborn, and he returned Mason's calm gaze with increasing hostility. For a moment Mason thought he might give them something, a piece of important information that would point them in the right direction. Then the teen's expression became stonelike.

"Your enchiladas won't take long," he ground out through set teeth. "I'll bring them out as soon as they're ready."

He left abruptly, and disappeared behind a swinging door in the far wall. Mason spared a hope that he hadn't angered the kid enough that he'd do something disgusting, like spit on his enchiladas.

Karina watched him go, then turned a satisfied grin toward Mason. "See? Nobody who knows Alex would ever think he could do something like that."

Mason stared after the kid. Unfortunately, he got the impression the boy was simply defending a friend, not speaking from specific knowledge. If there was something behind his denial besides loyalty, he was hiding it better than Mason thought he could.

"Too bad," he remarked to Karina.

"What do you mean?"

He picked up his water glass and sipped from the straw. "I don't care how many of his buddies insist Alex wouldn't hurt José, it's going to take more than a few character witnesses to clear him of murder charges. We need someone who saw them that night."

She sagged against the chair back, shoulders slumped. Mason felt a stab of guilt. He hated to pop her bubble, but she needed to be realistic. With the evidence the police had against Alex, even though it was circumstantial, Mason would have to come up with something pretty substantial to convince the judge to release him.

"Sorry." He reached across the table and covered her hand. "But don't lose hope. We've hardly begun. We'll come up with something soon."

She rewarded him with a grateful smile, and didn't move her hand. Mason sat there, his arm extended across the table, his fingers growing warm where they touched her skin, reluctant to pull back and break the moment. It was almost as if years had fallen away, and she was looking to him to solve her problems, to be the strong one and provide the support she needed. He liked the feeling.

Finally she slid her hand out from beneath his and placed it in her lap. Her gaze didn't quite meet his.

"Do you have any ideas?"

The truth was, he didn't. But he had more than an idea. He had a suspicion. And he knew where to go to figure out if that suspicion would pan out.

"Yeah, the name's Maddox." Mason spoke into his cell phone while they crossed the parking lot toward the rental car. "M-A-D-D-O-X. Russell."

"You know, you could do a simple internet search yourself."

Brent, his friend and the third member of the Falsely Accused Support Team, sounded like he was standing right beside Mason, thanks to the ridiculously expensive and super fancy phone he'd insisted they all carry. Brent was the geek of the group, and owned every gadget on the market.

"I could," Mason agreed, "if I had access to a computer, but we're getting in the car at the moment."

"Use your smartphone," Brent said.

Mason held the phone away and examined the screen for a moment, then shook his head. "I can't even figure out how to stop dialing the thing with my ear while I'm trying to talk on it."

Brent heaved a loud sigh, obviously for Mason's benefit. "Okay, fine. What am I looking for?"

They arrived at the car, but Mason waved Karina away from the door. "If I knew, I wouldn't need you to look for me. Just find out whatever you can about the guy. And see if there's a connection to a little dive called Casa del Sol Restaurante, or to—" He spoke to Karina. "What's the name of the place Alex works?"

"The Speedy Superette on Chacoma."

He spoke back into the phone. "Did you hear that?"

"Yeah, I got it." A pause. "Okay, give me a bit. Lauren and I are over at my sister's, so I'll call you back later."

"Thanks, buddy." Mason disconnected the call and spoke to Karina while he pocketed the phone. "Do me a favor and stand over there."

"Why?" she asked as she moved to the place he'd pointed, twelve feet across the parking lot.

"Just in case."

Concern creased her brow and she stood clutching the strap of her handbag, watching him closely. Mason approached the rental car with a cautious step. He stooped down and looked below, but could see nothing unusual about the undercarriage, nor was there anything hidden behind the wheels. They'd been in the restaurant for over half an hour, far longer than they'd been in the Garcias' house. If whoever cut the gas line on Karina's car *had* intended to blow them up, they might decide to go bigger with a second attempt.

With a breath captured in his chest, he pushed the remote to unlock the door. An audible *click* sounded, and the headlights flared to life. With his arm extended at full length and his head turned away—the right side toward the car, since a second blast would at least give him a matching set of singed ears—he opened the door. Encouraged, he stooped down and pulled the hood release lever.

Stomach muscles taut, he moved to the front of the car and lifted the hood. At least they'd parked beside a light pole that shed a little light, though much of the engine's interior lay in shadows. Was there an explosive device hiding down in there? He pulled the phone out of his pocket. If they'd *really* wanted to make this thing handy, they would have built a flashlight into it. As it was, he slid a finger around the screen until it lit up, and then used the light to inspect the engine. He found the gas line and checked it by feel. No cuts.

"I think it's all right," he called to Karina.

She approached, her expression grateful, and paused before she slid into the passenger seat. "Thank you, Mason."

He looked at her across the hood. "For what?"

A tiny smile curved her lips. "For keeping me safe."

A quippy reply danced on the tip of his tongue, something about self-preservation and not wanting to get the other side of his face blown off, but it died at the sight of that sweet smile. Keeping her safe felt natural, and satisfying in a way that was faintly disturbing. So he made no answer at all.

They seated themselves in the car, and clicked their seatbelts. When the engine started smoothly, they both exhaled relieved sighs they'd been holding, then exchanged a grin at their shared paranoia. The dashboard display announced the time as almost nine o'clock. He'd really like to find out if the investigating officers had discovered any witnesses when they'd questioned the neighbors around the Garcia residence. But Grierson had probably warned them off talking to him, and Parker's date was no doubt in full swing at the moment. Talking to him would have to wait until the morning.

He needed to find a hotel for the night, though he wasn't too keen on sitting alone all evening the first night back in Albuquerque. Those ghosts Caleb mentioned were bound to haunt this night. The longer he could put that off, the better.

He glanced sideways where Karina was smoothing her thick hair back into its band. "You mentioned something about being able to fix my hair so I don't look like a bombing victim. Want to give it a try?"

"Sure. My apartment's not far." She pointed at the street bordering the parking lot. "Turn right here, and then take the third left."

Her apartment. And with Alex in juvy, they'd be alone.

Warning Klaxons sounded in his head as he shifted into Drive and headed in the direction she'd indicated.

TEN

The feel of Mason's hair was so familiar it almost hurt Karina to touch him. How many times had she cut his hair over the years? She knew the way it grew, the slightly uneven hairline above his forehead, the almost-cowlick behind his right ear. Steeling her jaw against a tremble, she forced herself to maintain an impassive expression and tested the length between her fingers.

"Been a while since you had it cut?" Thank goodness her voice came out evenly despite the tide of emotions that swelled inside her.

"Yeah, I guess I'm about due."

He sat in the chair she'd set in the center of her small kitchen, a black stylist's apron secured around his neck. She ran a comb experimentally across his head, carefully avoiding the burned area above his left ear where the hair had singed down to the scalp.

I'll pretend it's a random haircut from a walk-in customer. Joe Blow, who strolled in for a trim.

She slid her clippers from their black case and plugged them into the wall outlet above the counter.

"Who's been doing your hair?" Not that she really wanted to know, but if she kept him talking about impersonal things, maybe she could forget whose head she was caressing.

"Nobody in particular. There's a place not far from my house I go to. Seems like I get a different stylist every time I go in there."

She reached for a guard, and then hesitated, her fingers hovering over them. "You know it's going to have to be pretty short, right?"

Mason waved a hand beneath the apron. "Shave it if you have to."

"I don't think we need to be quite that drastic."

She picked up a number three, attached it and flipped the switch. The clippers hummed to life. With her teeth set together, she tilted his head and started running the clippers across his scalp against the direction of growth. Hair fell to the floor with each swipe.

"So do you still go to Trinity?" He raised a hand to point at the framed watercolor hanging on the wall above the entryway.

The picture was of a plain wooden cross suspended above a filled baptismal. She'd painted it during high school art class, working from a snapshot Mason had taken of their church's sanctuary.

"Not anymore." She bent down to position the clippers at a good angle at the nape of his neck. "Alex and I go to Cornerstone Christian now."

Trinity Community Church. When Mason moved

away, she'd considered returning to the church where they'd met at youth group during their sophomore year in high school. But the memories were too vivid, too painful. Every time she walked into the sanctuary she couldn't focus on the Lord, because Mason's presence was everywhere.

"What about you?" she asked. "Where do you go to church these days?"

"I don't." His answer was brief, clipped.

Surprised, she paused and held the clippers a few inches from his head. "You don't attend church at all?"

Mason had been an enthusiastic Christian during high school and college. Seeing his commitment had deepened her relationship to the Lord, and to the church. They'd even gone on a mission trip to Mexico with their youth group the summer after their senior year.

"Not anymore." His mouth snapped shut, the brittle line of his lips announcing that he wouldn't discuss the subject any further.

Karina continued combing through his hair with the clippers. What had happened to him? In the next moment she realized she knew the answer. Margie. His wife's death must have created some sort of crisis of faith for him.

But, Mason, surely you don't blame Jesus for what happened to Margie.

The words were on the tip of her tongue, but she swallowed them. Some topics were too far beyond her ability to discuss calmly, and Mason's wife was one of them.

After all, hadn't she suffered her own crisis of faith when he broke up with her to marry Margie? Karina and Mason had been together for years, since early high school. They'd loved each other. Even now she did not doubt that. But they'd been young, and their relationship had grown predictable, too comfortable. They both knew it, but neither had admitted it to the other. When he'd proposed to her, she'd been overjoyed with the tiny promise ring he'd given her and had hoped it would renew the depth of the passion that had begun to cool. But then he'd met Margie. Bigger than life, vibrant, beautiful Margie.

She finished the cut in silence. As she worked, Mason's face clouded over with painful memories, his thick brows sunk low over his eyes. Was he thinking of her, his dead wife? Karina clamped her teeth together. She should have kept her mouth shut. The last thing she wanted was for Mason to brood over his wife while sitting in her kitchen.

When she'd finished the clip, she removed the guard and trimmed a clean line at the back of his neck and around his right ear. The burned left ear she left alone. Then she unsnapped the apron and removed it from his neck, careful to trap the hair fragments in its flimsy folds.

"There. All finished." She pointed toward the bathroom a few feet away, down a short hallway. "Go take a look and see what you think."

When he left the room, the atmosphere became noticeably lighter. Karina retrieved her broom from its storage place in the pantry and began cleaning the floor.

Mason returned within a minute and stood in the doorway. "It's terrific. Thank you."

She looked up at him, and her breath caught in her chest. The shorter hair transformed him. Stubble across his jaw gave him a rugged look. And the short hair did something to make his eyes stand out. They were so bright blue it almost hurt to look at them, like looking into the sun. Those were the eyes she'd gazed into countless times, had lost herself in. Had planned to look into for the rest of her life.

Until he broke her heart into a million pieces.

She tore her gaze away and turned to retrieve the dustpan. "You should wear your hair short all the time. That style looks good on you."

"Feels good, too." He ran a hand across his head. "Here, let me get that."

He took the dustpan from her and knelt at her feet, holding it in front of the pile of dark hair. In a flash, Karina remembered another time Mason knelt before her. That time he'd held a ring in his fingers. Pain squeezed her throat shut.

With an iron effort she swept the hair into the dustpan, then nodded toward the cabinet beneath the sink, where the trash can stayed. She turned her back on him to put the broom away and spoke over her shoulder. "So where are you staying tonight? Did you make reservations somewhere?"

There was no answer, but the weight of his stare burned into the back of her head. With purposefully smooth movements, she put the broom away and shut the door before turning to look at him.

Something smoldered in those blue eyes. Something intimate and familiar.

"I was thinking maybe I should crash on your couch." He moved his head in the direction of the living room and the sofa, but didn't break the eye contact that held her captive. "You know. Some extra protection for you."

What was he saying? Her pulse kicked up speed. Was he offering more than simply a protective presence for the night? The Mason she had known years ago would never suggest such a thing. He was too dedicated to the Lord, too determined to save himself for marriage. But that Mason was gone, and this man—this very attractive man—was someone she didn't know. She couldn't decide if she liked him or not. At times today she'd hated him for his casual, sarcastic tongue. At other times she appreciated his rough but thorough concern for her. And this evening she found herself strangely drawn to him. Which made him dangerous.

And yet, she *was* afraid to be alone. The day's events had terrified her. What if the big man in the black car came back? What if whoever was responsible for burning her car decided to pay a visit to her apartment?

At the thought of Mason sleeping on her sofa all night long, just a few feet beyond her bedroom door, a desert invaded her throat.

Lord, I need You! Please help me.

The prayer, an unspoken connection to Heaven, gave her a tendril of strength. Drawing on reserves of calmness she didn't possess on her own, she replied in an even tone.

"You can't stay here, Mason."

Something flashed in those piercing blue eyes. Regret, perhaps? In a moment it was gone, and the smug grin returned.

"I figured you'd say that. It was worth a try, though."

What was that supposed to be, an insulting comment? The insinuation that she might have relented, that a night on her couch might have led to something else, created an instant fury inside her. She drew herself upright, ready to pounce back with a verbal volley, something about him being the last man on earth she'd want sleeping on her couch no matter how much danger she was in, but the words went unspoken. Because at that moment his cell phone rang.

Straightening, he slid it out of his hip pocket and glanced at the screen.

"My friend in Atlanta." He clipped the words short while he stabbed at the screen, then lifted the phone to his ear. "What have you got for me, Brent?"

His eyes went distant for a moment as he listened,

and then a slow smile curved his lips. He didn't lower the phone, but spoke to her. "Bingo."

Karina's pulse kicked into overdrive for the second time in as many minutes.

"At first it looked like I'd run into a dead end."

Mason spared a moment to marvel at the technology of the small rectangle resting on the table between them. The quality of his voice through the phone's speaker was nothing short of amazing. Not a trace of the tinny quality of most speakerphones. If Mason closed his eyes, he could almost picture Brent sitting right beside them in Karina's tiny kitchen instead of talking through a cell phone.

"Casa del Sol Restaurante is owned by a private company called Alimento Sabroso."

Karina supplied the translation without raising her eyes from the phone. "That means *flavorful food*."

"The outfit owns another restaurant there in Albuquerque called, predictably, Casa del Luna. You know—sun, moon. Anyway, the primary owner is listed as Jorge Sastrias."

Mason's ears pricked. Their waiter had said that he never got to wait on Maddox, because Jorge always took care of him personally. He addressed the phone. "You said primary owner?"

"That's right. Mr. Sastrias has a partner, another corporation. This one's called Good Food Enterprises. Good Food also owns an interest in a half-dozen or so other restaurants in Albuquerque and Santa Fe, but only the two with Mr. Sastrias."

"O-kay." Mason processed this information. "So who owns Good Food Enterprises? Maddox?"

A chuckle sounded through the phone. "Not so fast. There's no single owner listed. Good Food Enterprises is a subsidiary of a corporation called Grayscale Incorporated."

Karina shook her head. "Wait a minute. I'm confused."

"Now you're feeling my pain," Brent said. "It's like an endless chain of corporations. Trying to track them down is like following one of those pencil mazes. But the trail ended at Grayscale. And guess who's the chairman of the board of Grayscale Incorporated."

Mason didn't need to guess. He knew. With an effort, he managed to say the name without spitting. "Russell Maddox."

"Exactly. And guess who owns Powerhouse Fitness."

Mason didn't bother to state the obvious. Instead, Karina did. "Grayscale?"

"Right again. It's one of the few businesses owned outright by Grayscale."

Mason drew the next line himself. "Let me guess. One of the other businesses is the Speedy Superette."

"Nope. That would be too easy, wouldn't it?"

He arched his eyebrows and looked across the table at Karina, who looked as surprised as he felt.

"Good Foods, maybe?" she asked.

"That would make sense, wouldn't it? But no."

Brent's voice warmed. He was obviously enjoying making them wade through the process he'd followed to trace this information. Mason bit back an impatient suggestion that his buddy cut to the chase and just tell them what he'd discovered.

Karina was apparently okay playing Brent's guessing game. "Is it Mr. Velesquez, Alex's boss?"

"That's partly right. It's the same sort of setup as the restaurant. Benito Velesquez is the primary owner, in partnership with a company called Albuquerque Connections, Inc. And *that* company is a subsidiary of Landwise Associates, which also owns a realty company and a real estate management company."

Mason tapped his fingers impatiently on the table. A guy needed to draw a map just to keep it all straight. "So how does that lead back to Grayscale?"

"It doesn't."

Karina jumped when he slapped his hand flat against the plastic tablecloth and a loud smack filled the room. He glared at the phone. "I thought you said you found a connection."

Brent's laughter sounded in sharp contrast to Mason's frustrated tone. "Calm down, dude. Landwise Associates has a board of directors, too."

He paused, but Mason refused to swallow the bait. He kept his teeth clamped together.

Karina asked the question Brent was obviously

fishing for. "Is Russell Maddox the chairman of that board as well?"

"No. It's better than that." Brent paused, then delivered the tidbit. "The chair*woman* of the board is named Olivia Sullivan Maddox. Otherwise known as Mrs. Russell Maddox."

Moving together, Karina and Mason both sat back in their chairs and let the news sink in. Maddox partially owned the restaurant where José had worked, and his wife owned the grocery store where Alex worked.

"There's more." Brent was enjoying this way too much, judging by the delight in his tone. "I found a couple of news articles referring to Mrs. Maddox as an invalid, so I did a little digging into her background. Apparently she had an accident almost ten years ago that left her paralyzed and bedridden. She still holds her position on the Landwise Associates board of directors, but she defers all decision making to... Want to take a guess?"

This time Mason spoke, but it was no guess. "Her devoted husband."

"You got it." A loud, satisfied sigh sounded through the speaker. "There's your connection."

Mason's finger tapped a yellow spot on the tablecloth while he digested the information Brent had unearthed. The pieces were all present, but there were so many layers it was hard to make sense of the whole.

After a moment Brent's voice broke the silence. "Listen, it's after midnight here and I have an eight o'clock meeting in the morning. Do you need anything else from me?"

Mason jerked out of his musing. "No. You've been a big help. Thanks, dude. I owe you."

Laughter sounded through the speaker. "You sure do. I had to cut short an evening with my gorgeous wife to play computer jock for you. But don't worry. I'll find a way for you to return the favor someday."

"I'm sure you will." Mason grinned as he disconnected the call. He was so fortunate to have a guy like Brent as a F.A.S.T. partner, and especially as a friend.

Karina placed folded hands on the table and leaned forward toward him. "I don't understand the purpose of all those companies. Why doesn't Maddox just have one corporation that owns everything?"

"Distance," Mason answered. "He isn't hiding the fact that he's involved in them, but to know it, someone would have to dig for it."

She shook her head, confusion creasing her forehead. "But why?"

He pursed his lips, his brain busily trying to come up with reasons. Maddox was involved in something illegal, of that he was certain. But he'd been certain four years ago, too. Then it had been a hunch. Now he had a little more to go on, but not much.

There were only two reasons to put so many layers between an owner and a business operation. First, to lengthen the connection. If his name was not easily associated with a business, then he wouldn't be immediately held responsible by public opinion if something went wrong. An accusation of food poisoning, maybe, or a dispute with a renter. If a highly visible person like Maddox was identified as the owner, the press would be all over even an insignificant situation and turn it into a circus. The information was there, a matter of public record, but someone would have to do research to find it.

The only other reason Mason could think of was to share blame if something went wrong. If he had a couple of partners in every corporation, there were a lot of people Maddox could point his finger at, people who had far more day-to-day dealings with managing the businesses.

Karina waited patiently, her expression expectant.

"I can think of only two reasons," he finally said. "And both of them point to some sort of illegal activity." He rubbed a hand across his mouth, shaking his head. "The problem is, I have no idea what."

ELEVEN

At nine-fifteen on Wednesday morning, a knock sounded on Karina's door. Nerves taut after a long and anxious night during which she'd jumped at every noise in the area surrounding her apartment, she lifted a slat on the mini-blind and peeked outside. The sight of Mason's rental car should have relieved her. Instead her temper flared. He was forty-five minutes late.

She swung the door open with one hand, the other planted on her hip, and greeted him with a glare. His pleasant expression wilted the moment he caught sight of her face.

"What's wrong with you?"

"You said you'd be here at eight-thirty." The words ground out through gritted teeth.

He lifted a shoulder, obviously unconcerned. "Sorry. I overslept." The insolent smirk he'd worn much of yesterday returned. "You can deduct an hour from the generous fee you're paying me."

Of course he would take the opportunity to remind

her that he was doing her a favor. Her temper flared beyond the point of control.

"I should have remembered what I used to do. If I wanted you to be on time, I'd tell you to be there an hour earlier."

"And I should have remembered what a foul temper you have early in the morning."

The comment stirred her irritation even further, but while she was trying to come up with an appropriately scathing reply, her phone rang. She swung the door open wider and left him to close it while she headed for the kitchen and her phone. During the short distance, her conscience raised its head. Mason was right. Mornings were not her favorite time of the day. Never had been. Especially after she'd spent the entire night expecting a huge, scary man to kick her door down and murder her in her own home.

But that wasn't Mason's fault. Why did he seem to bring out the worst in her? He really was doing her a huge favor by flying to Albuquerque at his own expense. The least she could do was act grateful.

Lord, I need Your help here. He's Your child, and I know You love him. Help me not to want to slap his face every time he gives me that annoying smirk.

She reached for the phone, but before she pressed the button to answer the call, she cast a quick glance at him.

"I'm sorry. I didn't mean to snap. It was a long night." Without giving him a chance to reply, she pressed the button. "Hello?"

An unfamiliar voice on the other end. Male. "Is this Karina Guerrero?" Though there was no hint of an accent in his English, her name rolled off the man's tongue with all the appropriate emphasis, as only someone fluent in Spanish would do.

"Yes, it is."

The high, thin voice continued. "Ms. Guerrero, my name is Hector Navarro. I'm an attorney, and I've been assigned to your brother's case."

Hope washed away any residual irritation. She whirled and caught Mason's eye as she answered. "Yes, Mr. Navarro. I'm so glad Judge Carter finally assigned my brother an attorney."

Mason's eyebrows arched, and she awarded him an excited smile.

"The juvenile court dockets are overflowing, so it sometimes takes a while." She heard papers shuffle in the background. "I understand you are Alexander's legal guardian?"

"That's right."

"I've been reading over his file, and I'd like to go down and talk to him this morning. Because he's a minor, I'll need you to either be present or give me permission to speak with him alone."

She glanced at the clock on the microwave. The morning traffic should be winding down by now. "I can be there by ten."

"Perfect. I'll meet you there."

The call ended. She cupped the phone in her hand

and spoke to Mason. "We're supposed to meet him at juvy in forty minutes."

He made a show of looking at his watch. "Gee, looks like I'm right on time, huh?"

That comment would have irritated her ninety seconds before, but now she was able to smile. The situation suddenly didn't look so dire. Finally Alex would have legal representation, someone to help them prove his innocence.

"Let me grab my purse."

Mason parked the car in a space directly in front of the building. He glanced at the place where the black Impala sedan had sat yesterday. Hopefully the goon wouldn't risk a second attempt in broad daylight, especially in front of a row of windows with police officers on the other side.

His call to Parker on the way to Karina's house this morning hadn't been very enlightening. Parker hadn't been to work yet, so he didn't know anything about the car fire.

"What have you stepped in, buddy?" his old partner had asked.

"I don't know, but it sure stinks. It looks like your 411 about gang activity is accurate, no matter what Karina thinks."

"The family is always the last to know," Parker had replied. "I'll check the report, ask a few questions and give you a call back. In the meantime, stay low, okay?"

"You know it."

Mason had hung up feeling better about their chances of discovering something helpful. Parker was a terrific ally, with access to information Mason could never get on his own. Not anymore, anyway.

He hadn't mentioned Maddox to his former partner, though. He'd started to, but something had stopped him. A hesitation down deep. Four years ago, Mason had been positive that Maddox was somehow responsible for Margie's death. Parker had remained unconvinced, and had even gently suggested that Mason was letting his personal situation interfere with his judgment. Well, yeah. Who wouldn't? Try though he might, he could never convince Parker of Maddox's involvement. If he brought the guy's name up now, Parker would probably think he was simply nursing a grudge.

Heck, maybe he was. But it was a grudge based on gut instinct, and he intended to dig up some hard facts before he said a word against the person who was arguably the most powerful man in New Mexico.

And who knew? If he could tie Maddox to José's death, he might uncover something about Margie's death as well.

A man stood just on the other side of the metal detector, watching dispassionately as they passed through the frame. Mason took his mettle at a glance. Young, probably barely out of law school. Short, slender, and dressed in a dark gray suit one size too big for him. The jacket cuffs brushed his knuckles, and the hem of his trousers lay wrinkled atop his polished black shoes like an elephant's ankles.

A rookie. What else?

Mason schooled his expression as he emptied his pockets into a white plastic bowl, then followed Karina through the frame that looked like a doorway to nowhere.

"Ms. Guerrero?" the young guy asked, a polite and faintly dispassionate expression on his face.

"Yes." Karina's answer was pathetically eager. "Mr. Navarro?"

"Call me Hector." He offered a slender hand, which she shook. Then his polite gaze fixed on Mason. "And you are?"

"Mason Sinclair. A friend of the family." Mason attempted to shake the man's hand, but instead found his fingers encased in a delicate grip, his hand shaken once and then released.

Mason disliked him instantly.

A polite smile tightened the man's thin lips. "I'm afraid I'll have to ask you to wait outside while I speak with Ms. Guerrero and Alexander."

Karina rushed in. "It's okay. Mason is a close family friend, and I've asked him to sit in on our conversation."

The news appeared to hit Navarro like a lead pipe upside the head, but he managed to contain himself. His gaze flicked toward Mason's face, but never quite connected. "All right. If you say so."

With that he turned and headed toward the doorway, beyond which lay the visiting rooms.

*What a jerk. He doesn't want me around because
he's afraid of being caught out as an amateur.*

Mason managed a confident smile for Karina, and
gestured for her to follow the attorney.

They were led to a different room than the day before, identical to the other even down to the plastic
chairs. The guard let them in and left them alone for
a few minutes. Then another guard brought Alex in.
Mason and Hector averted their eyes while Karina,
crying quietly, embraced her brother.

Then they broke apart and Alex gave Mason a
guarded, jerky nod of greeting.

Karina looped a hand through her brother's arm
and tugged him toward the lawyer. "Alex, this is Mr.
Navarro, your attorney."

The kid towered over the little man, and Mason bit
back a smug grin at the way Navarro had to tilt his
head back to look the fourteen-year-old in the face.
He couldn't help notice that Hector gave Alex's hand
the same smarmy little four-fingered shake.

The attorney took immediate charge and pointed
toward a chair pushed beneath the table. "Have a seat,
please. I have several other clients to meet with, so
I'd like to get on with this."

Get on with this. Mason clamped his teeth together
on a sarcastic reply about brusque public defenders
who don't bill their clients by the hour. He selected
a seat across the table from Karina and Alex, and

scooted the chair away from the table to create a distance between himself and the others. In this conversation he'd be an observer, not a participant. After all, he wasn't here in any official capacity.

Hector set his briefcase on the floor and fished a slender folder out, which he opened on the table in front of him. Then he extracted a spiral-bound notebook, the kind kids bought at a department store for twenty cents apiece during the back-to-school sale, opened it to a clean page and poised a pen above it, ready to write.

"Alex, I've read the police report, but I'd like you to tell me what happened last Friday night."

Haltingly Alex recounted the same tale he'd given Mason the day before. Exactly the same, even using the same phrases and words.

Almost as if he'd rehearsed it. Interesting.

Mason steepled his fingers and held them in front of his mouth, his chin resting on his thumbs, and studied the kid as he talked. Though the delivery was a little smoother today—he'd had a couple of chances to grow comfortable with the tale, after all—it was still obvious to him that Alex was lying right up to the part where he insisted he didn't kill his friend.

Throughout the entire monologue the attorney never looked up from his note taking. His pen hurried across the paper leaving a scribbled trail of blue ink. Three full pages of it.

He's recording Alex's story word-for-word.

For some reason that irritated Mason even further.

Though it made perfect sense to take notes rather than record a session with a client and risk someone getting hold of the tape, the guy was missing half the conversation. Even people who hadn't been trained in interrogation techniques understood about body language, didn't they? Seventy percent of a person's meaning was relayed through nonverbal means. Facial expressions, the position of the hands, the way someone's shoulders were angled either toward or away from the person they were talking to—those all said far more than words, even to an untrained eye.

Not only was Alex's body sending some contradictory messages, but Hector's body was practically screaming. It was saying, "Yeah, whatever. I don't really care what you say, and I'm not paying much attention. I'll do the job I've been paid to do, but don't expect me to get personally involved."

By the time Alex finished, his arms were folded tightly across his chest and he had scooted around in his chair until his back was pressed against the hard plastic to put as much distance between the attorney and himself as possible. *He doesn't trust him. Smart kid.* Beside him, Karina watched the scribbling pen with an almost trancelike stare.

Navarro kept writing for almost a minute after Alex finished, then set his pen down. He finally looked up into his client's face. "All right. I'll contact the district attorney's office and find out how they're going to proceed. Then we'll make plans from there."

He tore the pages from the spiral notebook, laid them in the folder, and closed the flimsy cardboard cover.

Karina sat upright in her chair. "Wait a minute. That's it?" Her head turned to glance at Alex for a second, and then back to the lawyer. "What are we going to do *now?*"

Hector slid the folder back into his briefcase and answered without looking at her. "I told you. I'll speak with someone at the D.A.'s office and we'll figure it out from there."

"But does Alex have to stay here? What about bail or something?"

"We can't even ask the judge for a bail hearing until he gets more information from the D.A." The man got to his feet. "I promise I'll get in touch with you soon. Hopefully by the end of the week."

"The end of the *week?*" She cast a glance across the table at Mason, though what she expected him to do, he couldn't imagine. Much as he hated to admit it, the guy was right. The judge wouldn't release a kid with suspected gang involvement without knowing more details. Still, Navarro could pretend to be more sympathetic, the little jerk.

Mason didn't bother to get to his feet, though Karina and Alex did. Looking shell-shocked and a lot younger than he had ten minutes before, Alex let his attorney shake his fingers.

"Alexander, I promise you, I'll do everything I can to move this along as quickly as possible. In the meantime, the best thing you can do is be cooperative and get along with everyone here. If you cause trouble, word will get back to the judge." He paused and waited for Alex to look at him. It was the first time Mason had seen the little weasel look the kid in the face. "Do exactly as you're told and everything will work out okay. Do you understand?"

Though the advice to get along and be cooperative here was sound and completely logical, Mason was surprised by Alex's reaction. He jerked back like he'd been slapped, eyes suddenly round. The pair exchanged a long, weighty stare before the kid nodded.

Interesting. Something had just happened between the two, a private communication of some kind. Mason rested his elbows on the plastic arms of his chair, his mind busy.

Navarro waved at the window and the guard on the other side hefted himself out of the chair to open the door. The lawyer started to move toward it, then stopped suddenly as though he'd just remembered something.

"Oh, Ms. Guerrero, would you mind signing something?" Without even looking, he reached into his briefcase and slid out a sheet of paper. "It's a consent form for me to talk with Alexander without you being present."

He handed the paper to Karina and reached inside his jacket to whip a pen out of his shirt pocket. When Karina took it and headed toward the table to sign without a question, alarms sounded in Mason's head.

"Why would that be necessary?" Mason put weight

in his voice, so that the words filled the room and bounced off of the tile floor. Karina stopped with the pen above the paper, and Alex tossed a startled glance his way.

Navarro shrugged. "I don't see it as a necessity. Of course Ms. Guerrero will be privileged to anything I say to her brother. But if I'm in the building and have a few spare minutes, I can visit with him."

Karina opened her mouth to question him, and Mason could see by her expression that she was about to agree with the lawyer. He hardened his stare. Her brother was a minor. It was her responsibility to know everything that went on between him and his attorney. Besides, Mason didn't trust the little weasel.

Alex spoke up. "I'd like to have visitors whenever I can. It's pretty boring here."

Mason tried to catch Alex's eye, but the kid refused to look at him. To his disgust, Karina apparently came to a decision and signed the form. She cast a quick defiant glance toward Mason as she handed the paper to the public defender.

Dumb decision. He didn't bother to hide his disgust. He folded his arms and shifted his body in his chair so he was looking at the wall instead of her. Why was he wasting his time here anyway, if she wasn't going to listen to him?

"Thank you. I'll be in touch soon." Navarro tucked the paper away in his briefcase and left the room.

The moment the door closed, Karina rounded

on Mason. "What was that about?" The question sounded more like an attack. Which wasn't fair at all.

Mason gave her a cold look. "You're his *guardian*."

"Yes, and Hector is his attorney."

"You have a responsibility to be involved in Alex's defense every step of the way." He tried to stop himself from saying the next words, he really did. But the angry, accusing glare on her face goaded him. "Or have you forgotten the fact that one reason he's in this mess is because you weren't aware of what he was doing when he was running the streets in the middle of the night?"

Her face went white, and Mason instantly regretted the verbal barb. She felt guilty enough as it was, and only a jerk would remind her of that.

"I'm sorry." He softened his tone. "That was uncalled for. This isn't your fault. Really. You can't watch a teenager every minute. Nobody can."

Alex stepped forward, his face flushed. "In case you two haven't noticed, I'm right here. If you're going to talk about me like I'm some stupid baby who can't understand you, maybe I ought to just leave."

Mason tore his gaze from Karina's tortured face to look at the kid. "You're right, Alex. You're not a baby. You're a young man who's in a really ugly situation, and your sister is doing everything she can to get you out of it." He loaded unspoken meaning into his stare, Alex's request to protect Karina hanging in the air between them. "And I'm here to help her."

Alex took the meaning. His throat spasmed with

a swallow, and he jerked a nearly imperceptible nod. Then he turned to Karina. "I don't want you to do anything else. I've got an attorney now, and he'll take care of everything."

Karina visibly bolstered herself. "Of course I'm going to do whatever I can, Alex. You're innocent, and I'm not going to stand back and let you be accused of something you didn't do."

"No!"

The teen's vehemence surprised them both. Mason arched his eyebrows. Was that simply the protest of a brother concerned for his sister, or was there more behind Alex's shout?

The boy turned on Karina. "You need to just back off, you hear? My lawyer can handle everything. You don't know what you're getting involved with."

Outside the window the guard had noticed the altercation. He rose from his chair and started toward the door.

Mason spoke before the man could interrupt. "Why don't you tell us what's going on, Alex?"

The teen's face flushed a brilliant red. "Nothing's going on. I just want everybody to leave me alone, that's all."

A childish response, of course. Alex was clearly upset. Karina's mouth hung open, and the expression she fixed on her brother was both hurt and confused. But whatever she might have said was cut short when the guard opened the door and stepped into the room.

"Is everything okay in here?"

"I'm ready to go back to my room." Alex stomped past the man and was through the door before anyone could stop him.

Staring at his retreating back, tears sparkled in Karina's eyes. The sight of them made Mason want to run after the boy and drag him back here to apologize to his sister. Though in a part of his brain he knew the kid was trying to protect her from whatever he'd gotten himself mixed up in, he couldn't stand to look at the pain in her face. Even though she was the most infuriating woman in the entire world, he had to fight off an urge to round the table and gather her in a comforting embrace when the guard left them alone and followed Alex.

The impulse died in the next instant. She turned to him, fury burning in her face like a bonfire.

"This is all your fault! Calling you was the second biggest mistake of my entire life." She put both hands on the surface of the table and leaned forward, thrusting her face in his direction. "The first was getting involved with you when we were sophomores in high school. I wish I'd never met you!"

With that she stomped out of the room after the guard, leaving Mason to wonder why in the world he'd ever been stupid enough to return to Albuquerque.

TWELVE

"I have somebody else for you to check out, Brent. Name's Hector Navarro."

Mason paced the asphalt behind the rental car, one hand in his jeans pocket and the other holding his phone to his ear. Inside the car Karina sat like a statue staring through the windshield. Her stiff posture told him she was still unreasonably furious. The call to his F.A.S.T. partner had been partly to delay the moment when he had to climb into the seat beside her.

"Hold on a sec, Mason." Brent must have covered his phone, because his voice became muffled and distant as he spoke to someone else.

Mason paced from the rental car across several parking spaces, passed the bumpers of three other cars, then turned and retraced his steps. He'd just completed his third bumper-to-bumper trip when Brent returned to the conversation.

"Sorry about that. I was just finishing up a meeting. Now, tell me the guy's name again."

"Hector Navarro." Mason spelled the last name. "He's an attorney, a public defender. Looks like he's about twelve years old. The ink's probably still wet on his law degree."

A keyboard tapped in the background. "You think this Maddox guy's got a lawyer in his pocket?"

"No idea, but that's what I hope you can dig up," Mason replied.

"If there's a connection, I'll find it." A low chuckle rolled across the phone line. "Kind of funny, don't you think? When I was out in Vegas trying to help Lauren, you were back home researching stuff for me. Now the tables are turned, and I'm helping you and your girl."

Mason's feet skidded to a halt on the pavement. "She's not my girl. It is *not* the same thing."

A pause. "Okay, if you say so."

The indulgent tone in his friend's voice plucked at a couple of Mason's nerves. "Don't waste your time trying to draw parallels between my situation and yours. They don't exist. You were attracted to Lauren from the start and I'm—" A glance inside the car at Karina's statuelike silhouette set his teeth together. "I'm definitely not."

He must have sounded a lot fiercer than he thought, because Brent apologized. "My mistake. Sorry." But his voice didn't sound nearly contrite enough. "I'll get on this Navarro guy and call you back when I have something."

Mason disconnected the call without saying good-bye. Sometimes his friends could be even more ir-ritating than a meddlesome family. Caleb with his constant praying and Bible lessons, and now Brent's insinuations that there was something between Karina and him. It was enough to drive a guy nuts.

He headed for the driver's side. When he opened the door, he heard Karina's voice.

"I'll be right there, Lana. Thanks for letting me know." She closed the cover on her phone and looked up at him when he slid behind the steering wheel. Rather than the red-faced anger he'd expected, she looked a bit pale. "We need to go over to the salon right away." The words trembled on her voice.

"Is everything all right?"

She shook her head. "Someone broke in last night. My boss can't find anything missing, though. The only sign that anyone was there is my station." She swallowed. "It's been vandalized."

Karina pushed the hair salon's glass door open and rushed inside. Lana and Gloria were both there, working on customers. A familiar older woman sat in one of the chairs in the small waiting area, thumbing through a magazine. One of Lana's regulars, waiting for her weekly shampoo and style. Karina spared her a quick smile on her hurried way to her station. Mason followed at a slower pace.

"There you are, honey." Lana turned away from the woman in her chair to follow them, a pink curler in her hand. "I left everything the way it was so you could see it. Well, except for the apron, a'course. I moved that just to make sure…" She cast a quick glance toward her customer and went on in a near whisper. "To make sure there weren't no body under it."

Karina nodded, but Mason cocked his head, a quizzical expression on his face. "Why would you think that?"

Lana eyed him up and down, her expression going from curious to appreciative. Lana enjoyed talking with handsome men, and judging by her slow smile as she inspected Mason, he qualified.

"Aren't you gonna introduce me to your friend, honey?" Her eyes didn't leave Mason's face, though she addressed the question to Karina.

For some reason, her obvious delight in Mason disturbed Karina. Not that she was jealous. Of course not. She wasn't the slightest bit interested in Mason. Didn't even like him, in fact. He'd acted like an arrogant jerk with Hector, and for two cents she'd drive him back to the airport right now and dump him off to catch the next plane out of town. That settled in her mind, she made a quick introduction.

"Lana, Mason. Mason, Lana." She pointed at each as she said their name. When Lana's carefully plucked eyebrows rose, she expanded the introduction a bit. "Mason's a friend from long ago. And Lana's my boss."

Mason had apparently decided to change his stripes and pretend like he had some manners. He held out his hand for Lana to take. "I'm pleased to meet you. What were you saying about a body?"

Lana lingered over the handshake a moment too long, and Karina felt the unpleasant stirrings of jealousy. Which made her angry. Of course she wasn't jealous. If Lana wanted Mason she could have him, even though she was at least twenty years older than him. She'd been called a cougar before.

Still, Karina breathed a tad lighter when Lana released his hand and launched into a description of her morning. "I didn't see it when I first unlocked the door. My arms were so loaded with clean towels from home I near dropped them on the way to the back. It took me a few minutes to store them away, and then I come back up front. That's when I noticed it."

She paused and glanced at Karina's chair with the exaggerated gestures of a high school drama student. Though she'd already heard a version of this tale on the phone, Karina found herself caught up in the account.

"Noticed what?" asked Mason.

Lana's voice dropped to a harsh stage whisper. "The body in the chair." Then she smiled, and her voice returned to normal. "Not really, but it sure looked like one from the back. Somebody had taken one of the wig stands from up front and taped it to the chair. Then they tossed a couple of our aprons over it. From the back it looked like somebody was sitting there with a blanket over their head. Somebody who didn't move at all, like they was dead or something. It fell off when I jerked the apron away." She pointed at the chair, where a white plastic wig stand lay like a faceless, decapitated head. The curly brunette wig lay on the seat beside it. "That's when I noticed the mess."

They all looked at Karina's station. Her three drawers stood open and empty, and all her combs and curlers and spare shears had been piled on the small countertop beneath the mirror. The product bottles she kept on her shelf had also been added to the pile. What a weird feeling, to see her professional tools lying there in disarray. She'd always taken pains to keep everything neat and tidy at her station.

"Did you call the police?" Mason asked.

"Why, no." Lana shook her head. "Why should I? Nothing was missing. The rest of the store looks fine. We never leave anything in the register at night anyway, and besides, the door was still locked. I had to unlock it. I figured Karina musta come in after I closed last night looking for something, and maybe was playing a trick on me with the wig."

Karina shook her head absently while examining the jumble of products and tools. "I didn't, but even if I had, I would never leave a mess like this."

Mason glanced around the salon. "Who else has a key to the front door?"

"Just the two of us." Lana awarded a benign smile to Karina. "She's the only one I trust to open or close when I'm not here."

Karina returned the smile, but her insides were quaking. Why would someone break into the salon and not take anything? It didn't make sense.

"Is any of your stuff missing?" Mason nodded toward the desktop.

She didn't think so, but everything was a mess. Karina stepped up for a closer look at the jumble. When she did, her eyes landed on something she hadn't seen before. Peeking out from beneath a pile of rollers was the edge of a picture frame. Her gaze flew to the wall on the left of the mirror. In the place where her license normally hung was an empty space.

With her heart thudding in her throat, she reached into the mess with two fingers and tugged at the cheap frame. Curlers rolled off when she lifted it and she could see the front.

Chills raced up her spine and down her arms.

The glass covering her license was shattered, cracks spidering out from the center, where a pair of shears had been driven through the glass, the paper and into the cardboard backing. The scissors still stood there, the sharp tip embedded in glass—right through the middle of her name.

THIRTEEN

Once again Mason was subjected to an angry audience with his former boss. The second time wasn't any more pleasant than the first, especially with Karina's boss and a few customers standing in a cluster in the corner, watching with fascination. A uniformed police officer brushed fingerprint dust on the open shelves, hoping for a set of prints that Mason doubted he would find.

"Maybe you two didn't understand me yesterday." Grierson glared first at Karina, and then switched to him. "I thought I told you to stay out of this case."

Mason's spine was already as stiff as a corpse, so he couldn't stiffen any further. But he managed to bristle just the same. "You're suggesting that we somehow invited this vandalism? C'mon, Sergeant, that doesn't make sense."

The man's lips tightened. "It's detective, and yes, that's exactly what I'm suggesting. I might be tempted to think differently if the store had been robbed, or if anyone else's things had been messed with. But those." He pointed first at the plastic head and then at the scissors protruding from the picture frame, and his glare deepened. "This is clearly a warning to Ms. Guerrero and you. Unless you're involved in something else—which I wouldn't put past you—I have to assume the warning is related to her brother's murder charge."

Mason fumed at the man's accusatory manner. Any number of sarcastic comments vied for airtime on his tongue, but he deemed it wise to hold them back.

After a quick glance in his direction, Karina spoke up. "The only thing we did after we left you yesterday was have dinner and go back to my place." At Grierson's unspoken question, she flushed. "I cut Mason's hair, and then he went to his hotel."

Grierson looked at him. "Which is…?"

"The Motel 6 over on César Chávez, near the airport." He anticipated the next question and cut the detective off as he drew breath to ask it. "And no, I didn't go anywhere else. I checked in, went to my room and watched television until I fell asleep." He started to add that the desk clerk could verify his story, but didn't bother to state the obvious. Grierson most certainly would check his statement.

After an awkward moment during which Mason was subjected to one of the silent scrutinizing stares he remembered very well from his days on the police force, Grierson turned away from him to face Karina. Despite himself Mason released the breath of air he'd been holding captive in his lungs.

"Ms. Guerrero, what are you involved in?" He nodded toward the faceless head in the chair. "This kind of stuff doesn't happen without a reason."

"I have no idea, Detective. I promise. Unless, like you say, it has something to do with my brother."

Tears glistened in her dark eyes, but she returned Grierson's gaze without blinking. In spite of the harsh words spoken at the detention center that still hovered between them, Mason admired her unflinching self-possession in the face of Grierson's hard stare.

She'll make a terrific courtroom witness for Alex. Her honesty shows in her face, in her bearing.

Grierson apparently believed her, for the hard lines of his face softened. "I know how difficult this must be for you. You're frightened for your brother, and now it seems as though whatever he's involved with is also posing a threat to you."

Mason thought she might take offense to the detective's assumption that Alex was involved with something illegal—which even she would have to admit looked likely—but she didn't react, except that a tear slipped over the rim of one eye and rolled down her cheek. Deep inside Mason, something twisted in response. It was all he could do not to reach out and dry her cheek with a gentle finger.

"That's why it is so important that you talk to me, Ms. Guerrero. Not to your friends. To me. I need to know everything you know. Only if you're completely honest with me can I give you the protection you need, and your brother the help he needs."

He held her gaze with his, the strength of the connection between them so strong it was almost visible. Though he stood close enough that he could have touched either of them by leaning sideways, Mason felt like an outsider, like he might as well be in another room. He wanted to catch Karina's eye, to caution her against confiding anything to this man who had far more training and experience in investigative procedures than she, or even himself for that matter.

He doesn't really care. It's a ploy, a trick. He's making himself appear sympathetic in order to get information. And he's really good at it. Mason almost fell for it himself. The words were on the tip of his tongue, the information Brent had uncovered, his distrust of Alex's freebie lawyer. Grierson had always been a jerk, and had not believed in Mason's innocence during Margie's murder investigation, but he'd never seemed even the slightest bit crooked. Maybe they should trust him.

Karina broke the stare-down with a trembling smile. "Thank you, Detective. I really appreciate your wanting to help my brother. I wish I had something to tell you. But honestly I don't know what's going on. I can't imagine what anyone would want to warn me against."

Grierson held her gaze a moment longer, then nodded. "And you're positive nothing is missing?"

"Yes, I'm positive." Karina leaned back to see around the uniformed officer. Her eyes moved, and then a crease appeared in her forehead. "No, wait. There is something missing. My gloves."

"Gloves?" Mason asked. "You mean like a pair of winter gloves?"

"No, I mean like a pair of reusable latex gloves for coloring. Black."

Latex. Mason exchanged a glance with Grierson, and they both sighed.

"You're wasting your dust," Mason said to the officer. "You won't find any prints there. Your best bet is the door and the drawer handles." The vandal would have touched both of those before finding the gloves. But the door probably had thousands of prints since this was a public business, and the drawer handles were thin metal loops which any thief worth his salt would have opened with a pencil or something that wouldn't leave a print.

The officer paused, the bristles of his fiberglass brush poised above the head-shaped wig stand, looking to Grierson for direction.

The detective glared at Mason. "I'm giving the orders around here." Then he shifted his gaze to the officer and eked out an order that sounded like the words tasted bad in his mouth. "Go ahead and finish with that, but spend some extra time processing the door and the drawer handles."

Mason judged it wise to keep his face smirk-free.

Grierson turned back to Karina. "Try to stay out of trouble, Ms. Guerrero." He looked pointedly at Mason and then back at her. His meaning was clear.

Hanging around with Mason was definitely *not* staying out of trouble.

He started to walk away, but Mason stopped him. "Wait a minute. Is that all? Don't you think you should give her some extra protection?"

The man's lips went thin for a moment. "Not that it's any of your concern, but I've already decided to alert the officers who patrol the area around her apartment and here. They'll keep an eye out for anything unusual."

Mason shook his head. "Not good enough. She needs dedicated protection."

The detective blasted a laugh. "Out of the question. This clearly was not a threat on her life. It was harassment."

He could hardly believe his ears. "Somebody blew up her car yesterday. Was that just harassment too?"

His voice rang in the small beauty salon, and one of the customers watching from the corner let out a loud gasp.

Grierson's face took on the almost pleasant expression that Mason had long ago identified as his own peculiar brand of stubbornness. "The report on the car confirmed your suspicions that the fuel line was cut. That's why I'd already decided to increase patrol around her. Now I'll add additional patrol to her place of employment." He leaned closer and lowered his voice. "If I were going to request dedicated protection, the one person I'd insist on guarding her against is you, Sinclair. I don't care if you did just get into town yesterday. My gut tells me you're involved in whatever's going on, and you're poison."

He whirled and left the salon without waiting for a reply. Mason stood staring at his back through the front glass, his dislike for the man expanding by the second. The reference to Margie's death was obvious, and it soured in Mason's stomach like curdled milk. The guy had been a jerk then, and he was still a jerk now. But beneath the intense dislike Mason felt for his former boss was something else. Something stronger and even more sickening.

The guy might be a jerk, but what if he was right?

When all her belongings had been returned to their proper positions, Karina tackled the black fingerprint dust with spray cleaner and a cloth. She kept her back to Mason, who sat brooding in a chair in the waiting area, but couldn't stop snatching glances at him in the mirror. With his brows gathered and sunk down over his eyes like that, he projected a palpable wall of anger that dared anyone to approach. The customers who came into the salon for a haircut avoided the empty seat next to him. Even Lana had stopped giving him flirty glances.

Karina had felt bad for him when Detective Grierson practically accused him of putting her in danger. That wasn't fair. He was only here because she'd asked him to come. Even so, now that he was here she was sorry she'd ever called.

When had he become so hard to get along with?

As a teenager and young man he'd been charming and energetic, the one who attracted all the attention. Strangers talked with him freely, and most of the time he managed to turn the conversation to his faith in the Lord. Not obnoxiously or aggressively, but naturally. Almost matter-of-factly, because his relationship with Jesus was an integral part of his personality, of who he was. Had the loss of that faith turned him into this surly, suspicious man who trusted no one and seemed determined to make sure everyone knew it?

And yet, beneath the surly exterior, she had glimpsed the real Mason, the one she had fallen in love with. She saw him more and more, especially when the two of them were alone. Those glimpses gave her hope, and fed a flame she wasn't yet ready to admit existed.

"Honey, here you go. You can hardly tell at all."

Karina jerked herself out of her thoughts with a start. Lana had been doing something at the front desk, and now approached holding out a picture frame. Karina took it from her hand. It was her license. A crease wrinkled the letters of her last name and a missing chunk made it nearly unreadable, but other than that, the paper had been restored.

"I taped it from the back," Lana said. "At first I thought we might have to apply for another copy, but I think this one will be just fine."

Karina ran a hand over the edge of the black frame. "Where did you get…?" Her gaze fell on the wall next to Lana's station. The place where her license had hung was empty. Tears blurred her vision. "Oh, Lana."

The woman became brusque. "Now, don't take on. I have another frame at home, so it's not a big deal." She took the frame out of Karina's hand and stepped forward to hang it on the hook. Then she backed up to examine her handiwork with her head tilted to one side. "There. Now you're back to normal." She peered at Karina sideways. "Uh, you *are* coming back to work, aren't you? I mean, I'd understand if this put a bad taste in your mouth."

A guilty flush stained the woman's face. Karina rushed to allay her fears. "Lana, this isn't your fault. It's my fault." She stopped at the look of surprise on her boss's face, and shook her head. "I mean, not because of anything I've done. It has something to do with José's death, and Alex and I don't know what else." As she said the words, she realized that, in a way, she'd put Lana and her business in danger. Not by anything she'd done, but just by being employed here. Which was the last thing she wanted. "In fact, it might be better for you if I didn't come back to work for a while. There's always a possibility that whoever did this will come back, and the next time they might decide to trash more than my station."

She couldn't believe she was suggesting that she quit her job. Without the income this job provided— or more specifically, the tips her customers gave her—she'd sink financially. But neither could she be responsible for putting her boss in danger.

But Lana dismissed the idea out of hand. "Don't be sayin' anything of the kind. I've been meaning to call and have my alarm system turned back on. Shoulda done that a long time ago. And I've been thinking of maybe getting a dog, too. A big one that stays quiet during the day and barks a lot at night. I'd make him a bed right up front by the register, so anybody who walks by could look in the window and see him." She put out a hand and awkwardly patted Karina's arm. "I can't do without you, honey. The customers like you better than me."

Touched and relieved, Karina could only smile. "Thank you."

The door opened. Two ladies walked in, chatting together, and joined two others who sat with Mason in the waiting area.

"Speakin' of customers." She lifted her head and called in a cheery voice, "There's a little bit of a wait, but I'll get you in as soon as I can."

Karina glanced around the salon. "Where's Gloria?"

"Pppbt." Lana let out a disgusted raspberry. "That wimp. Said havin' the cops here aggravated her nervous condition, and she went home with a headache. I called Maria, but she can't get here until four. But don't worry. I can handle it."

Now it was Karina's turn to feel guilty. She couldn't leave Lana with a waiting room full of customers. And besides, what else was she going to do this afternoon? Exchange verbal darts with Mason?

"You know what? I'd like to stay." She grinned and said in a teasing voice that only Lana could hear. "I need to cut something. It'll help me let off some steam."

Relief lightened her boss's features. "Well, if you're sure."

"I am." Karina slid her gaze sideways, to where Mason sat slumped in his chair. "Just give me a minute."

She crossed the floor, smiling at the waiting ladies, and stood by Mason's chair. "Let's talk." Without waiting for an answer, she left the salon.

He followed, as she had known he would.

"I'm going to stay and work for a few hours," she said before he could speak.

A thoughtful expression crossed his features, and he nodded. "That's a good idea. It's a pretty visible place. Kind of boring, but at least the chairs are comfortable."

Karina shook her head. "I don't want you to stay. In fact, I think it would be best if you went back to Atlanta."

That surprised him. His lips parted, but no words came out for several seconds. It was the first time she'd seen him speechless since she'd picked him up at the airport yesterday.

The silence didn't last long. "Are you firing me?"

"Well…yes. I guess I am. I'm sorry I got you involved at all. I was feeling alone and overwhelmed." She looked up into a frigid smile.

"You can't fire me, Karina. You're not footing the bill, remember? I'm here on my own dime."

The reminder acted like a billows, and blew a spark of irritation into a full-fledged fire. Why could he stir her into anger so quickly? Normally she kept better control of her temper. *Stress. That must be it.*

Her teeth set together, she ground out a reply. "And I appreciate that, but I don't need you anymore."

With a maddening shake of his head he discounted her comment. "I don't agree. We're onto something with this Maddox connection. A little more digging and I'm sure I can come up with something that will prove Alex didn't kill his friend."

"His attorney can do that."

A scowl twisted his features. "That kid? He's barely old enough to drive, much less prove a case against a heavy hitter like Maddox."

The obvious disdain he held for Hector acted like sandpaper on a raw nerve. She folded her arms across her chest. "You were rude to him today."

"Yeah? Well, he hasn't done anything to earn my respect." His lips twisted into a disgusted smirk. "Sitting there like some kind of secretary taking shorthand. He never even looked at Alex, never asked a single question."

"He didn't have to," she snapped back. "Alex told him everything, and obviously Hector believed him. If we give him all the information your friend uncovered then he can—"

"Don't you dare!" Mason's shout made her jump.

"If it turns out he's on Maddox's payroll, you'll be giving it straight to the man himself. You might as well lie down in the middle of I-40 during rush hour."

"You have no reason to think Hector is on Maddox's payroll." She moved closer, her face inches from his, and forced him to look her in the eye. "What happened to you, Mason? You never used to be like this. You used to trust people."

His reply was bitter, even poisonous. "Yeah, and look what it got me. A dead wife."

If she hadn't been so close, she would have missed the almost silent intake of breath and the pain that darkened his eyes as the words hung, raw and naked, between them. He turned away, toward the parking lot, his gaze growing distant as he watched the cars driving by on the busy street beyond.

Her irritation with him vanished in an instant, replaced with an aching tenderness. *So that's it. He feels responsible.*

"Mason." She said his name softly, but he didn't turn to face her. "Margie's death was not your fault."

A long silence, during which she watched his eyes move back and forth tracing the line of traffic. When he did speak, he didn't look at her.

"What if it was?"

Beneath the words lay a hint at such pain as she couldn't even imagine. She'd finally uncovered the root of his sarcastic, bitter attitude. But how could he possibly feel responsible for his wife's murder? Her heart ached as though someone had slipped a knife inside her rib cage. What a heavy burden to bear alone.

She laid a hand on his arm. "You loved her, Mason. How could you ever be responsible for her death?"

Funny, but saying the words didn't hurt like she thought they would. All she could see was the pain etched in the lines on his face. She watched his profile, saw his throat move with a swallow before he whispered an answer.

"A week before she was killed, a man held up a liquor store. When Parker and I arrested him, he still had the weapon on him, a hunting knife. Got a positive ID on the guy and the knife from the clerk. We thought the conviction was a done-deal. But then out of the blue the district attorney dropped the charges because of—get this—lack of evidence. The clerk had changed his mind and wasn't sure about the guy after all." He shook his head. "We couldn't understand it. Parker wanted to move on, said we were trying to juggle too many live wires to go chasing a dead one. But it bugged me, you know? I couldn't let it go. I paid a visit to the clerk, pushed on him trying to find out why he reversed his story. All the guy would say was he couldn't be sure. But I knew he was lying."

The word flow stopped. His gaze grew even more distant, fixed somewhere in a painful past. Karina held her tongue, and after a minute, he continued.

"I should have listened to Parker and dropped it. But I kept pushing, looking for a reason. And then

I found it. The liquor store clerk showed up at work one day driving a brand new Mustang."

Karina couldn't stop herself. "Somebody paid him off?"

"Yeah. But why? Why would someone want to protect a common thief?" He shook his head, obviously still disturbed by the question. "I poked around, asking questions, doing research. But I never figured it out, because that's when…"

He stopped. Karina waited, but when it became apparent that he wasn't going to finish the sentence, she did.

"That's when Margie was killed."

A nod.

"And you think whoever was responsible for paying off the clerk killed her and blamed you to distract you from investigating further."

"I tried to tell Grierson that, but he didn't buy it." Anger flashed onto his face. "The idea that I killed Margie for the life insurance money was ridiculous. No amount of money would ever be worth losing my wife." His voice broke on the last word, and Karina watched tears fill his eyes. "When I got the check, I didn't even cash it. Just signed it over to charity. What could I buy with money that had come to me because of her death? I loved her *so much*."

In the silence that followed, he seemed to become aware of Karina's presence again. She realized that her hand still rested on his arm, and his skin had grown warm beneath her fingers. Hastily she removed it, and he cleared his throat.

"I'm sorry. You, of all people, shouldn't have to listen to me talk about how much I loved my wife."

"Mason, it's okay." As she said the words, Karina realized with a sense of wonder that she meant them. An unbidden smile curved her lips. For the first time ever, she was able to think of Mason and Margie's marriage without anger and hurt. Hearing him talk about his pain had worked as a healing balm. If for no other reason than this, having him come to New Mexico was worth the peace she now felt where Margie was concerned.

Thank You, Lord. I didn't know how much I needed to get rid of that bitterness. But You did.

"So anyway," Mason said, "that's why I'm not leaving."

His logic escaped her. "I don't understand."

He shifted his feet on the sidewalk to face her head-on. "Look, whoever killed Margie is still out there. And I know what they're capable of. Have you forgotten the size of that big goon who was watching you?"

A shudder shook her body. "No."

"Me neither. And since he showed up at your place before I even got here, that means he wasn't set on your tail because of me, so there's no reason to think he'll go away when I do. But I also think I might have stirred up some trouble since I arrived, and if that's the case, I'll be responsible if anything happens to you. I'm sticking around to make sure you're safe and Alex gets out of this mess in the clear. Grierson obviously holds some sort of grudge against me, and I'm sure that's why he didn't assign a full-time protective order for you. I'm all you've got." Something glimmered in his eyes. "And if I can prove that Maddox is somehow involved, so much the better."

The determination in his expression told Karina she'd never get him out of Albuquerque until this thing was over. And she was disturbed to discover that the idea of having Mason hanging around wasn't as repugnant as it had been a few moments before. In fact, something had seeped in to replace the bitterness that was now gone. Looking at him, warmth settled inside her, familiar and faintly exciting. With an effort, she pushed the feeling away. She could be his friend, but she would not let herself fall for him. Not again.

FOURTEEN

Sitting in the waiting room of a hair salon was, without exception, the most boring thing Mason had ever done. What was with all those women's magazines? Who cared about umpteen ways to tie a scarf? And did women really read articles about streamlining their beauty routines? Seriously? The chairs had been comfortable for the first hour or so. After that his backside grew numb and no amount of fidgeting or scooching helped. He paced every square inch of the small salon, examined every bottle on the shelves and learned more about controlling static hair than he ever wanted to know.

When he saw two police cruisers roll to a stop in the parking lot, he almost shouted with relief.

"I'm going to step outside," he hollered over his shoulder as he hightailed it through the doorway.

The officer who stepped out of the first car was a welcome sight.

"Parker. Hey, buddy. I was hoping you'd call, but this is even better."

His former partner returned his enthusiastic handshake. "I was going to, but then Grierson assigned us to extra patrol here, so I figured you'd be nearby. Thought I'd drop by and introduce you to my partner. This is Frank Graham. Frank, Mason Sinclair."

The man extended a hand and studied him with a calculating gaze. Mason resisted the urge to squirm. What tales had he heard about the ex-cop who'd been suspected of murdering his wife? Nothing bad from Parker, of that Mason was sure. But if he was Parker's partner, that meant he worked closely with Grierson.

Mason forced a cautious smile. "Good to meet you."

The man nodded, but said nothing. Just watched him with eyes that looked like they didn't miss much.

"So Grierson assigned you to keep an eye out for Karina?" he asked.

"Yeah. We've been told to step up our presence in this area, and keep an eye out for any unusual activity around her apartment, too. And if we see a black Impala sedan, we're to run the plates." Parker gave a snort. "I think he wanted to see my reaction when he told me you were in town."

"Well, whatever the reason, I'm glad you're on it. I can breathe easier." Mason glanced at Graham. Could he speak freely in front of the guy? "So, what's the scoop on the car fire yesterday?"

Graham didn't bat an eyelid when Parker answered without hesitating. Good. That meant he didn't mind Parker talking about the case. And apparently Parker trusted the guy, or he wouldn't talk in front of him.

"I talked to the investigating officers. They questioned everybody they could find up and down the street. Nobody saw a thing."

Mason shoved his hands in his pockets, digesting that information. "I find that hard to believe. The school bus had just come through. There were kids all over the place."

Parker agreed. "Apparently there were a couple of teenagers hanging around, and they were evasive the minute the officers approached. Insisted they'd been out in the yard a few doors down and didn't see anybody. Not a dark sedan, not a stranger, nothing."

Mason drew the obvious conclusion. "Covering for somebody."

"Yeah, that's what they figured. And one of them checked with the folks out at the auto yard. They haven't had time to go over the car thoroughly yet, but they said it was pretty obvious the gas line was cut, and that it could have been done from beneath."

"I figured that. Way too obvious to raise the hood of a car parked on the curb out in the open."

"It may even have been one of those teenagers. Nobody would give a second thought to someone from that neighborhood hanging around." An image of the street where the Garcias lived rose in Mason's mind. "The street was lined with cars. It's probably pretty common to see people working on them."

"That's what I figure, too," said Parker.

Graham said nothing. He sure was quiet. Mason glanced at his face, a feeling of unease settling over him. Didn't the guy ever talk? Or was he keeping his mouth shut because he disapproved of Parker talking to him about an open investigation? If so, would he report back to Grierson? Nah, probably not. Parker wouldn't speak so freely in front of him if he didn't trust him.

"What about this place?" Mason jerked a head toward the hair salon behind him. "You hear anything about that?"

"Just that there were scratches on the lock." A gruesome grin crept over Parker's face. "And that somebody rigged a head in a chair to look like a corpse. Pretty creepy."

"It was a wig stand," Mason told him. "But that wasn't as creepy as the scissors stabbed right through Karina's name on her license."

The grin faded, and Parker's expression became serious. "Yeah. I'm sure that freaked her out. So, buddy, what's your next move?"

Mason hesitated. Should he share Brent's findings about Maddox? Parker might trust Graham, but Mason didn't have any reason to. In fact, he still wasn't sure he wanted to bring up Maddox's name to Parker. Not until he had something more to go on.

He shrugged. "At this point I'm just hanging out and keeping my eyes open. We met Alex's freebie lawyer this morning. Guy named Hector Navarro. Ever heard of him?"

His former partner squinted as he thought, then shook his head. "Can't say I have. Why?"

"I don't like him," Mason replied instantly. "Young. No experience, as far as I can tell. Has the personality of a river rock."

Even Graham smiled at that comment. Parker put back his head and laughed. "Now, Mason. We were young and inexperienced once. We outgrew it, and so will he."

"Yeah, but I wish he'd earn his stripes on someone besides Alex."

Parker laughed again and clapped him on the shoulder. "I'm sure he'll be fine. We've got to get back on the street. You staying at my place tonight?"

Mason had fully intended to do that. He'd even checked out of the motel and stashed his stuff in the trunk of the rental car. But after this latest threat he was determined not to leave Karina alone in that apartment for the night.

"I appreciate the offer, but I think I'll hang around Karina's tonight."

A knowing smile settled over Parker's face. "I thought so."

Mason rushed to correct him. "It's not like that. Really. I just don't think she should be alone."

Parker slapped him on the back before moving toward his cruiser. "Whatever you say, buddy."

Graham, as stone-faced as ever, nodded a silent farewell and headed for his own car. Mason stood on the sidewalk and watched them leave. Trying to convince Parker that there was nothing between him and Karina would be a complete waste of breath.

His old partner had always been a ladies' man, and obviously that hadn't changed. He couldn't imagine being in the company of a beautiful woman and not trying his luck with her. Even though their past was stormy, Mason had too much respect for Karina to treat her so casually.

And yet last night while she was cutting his hair, he'd felt the stirrings of something. Not exactly a return of the old feelings. Something new and more than a little alarming. He'd felt it again this morning, when they'd talked about Margie.

What is going on between us?

One aspect of their former relationship had definitely revived. Friendship. In the Karina of today, Mason glimpsed more and more of his former friend. All the things that had attracted him to her initially— her quick mind, her easy acceptance of those she met, even her sharp tongue—were all still there. But there were differences. Now she had matured into a lovely woman.

If I hadn't met Margie...

He scrubbed at his scalp, trying to dislodge the disturbing thought. Yet the question had haunted him for so long. When he met Margie, he had been swept away in the excitement of new love. And he *had* loved her, truly, though their relationship had been different from his with Karina. Exciting and new and full of passion. They had been lovers, yes, but they had jumped so quickly into marriage they hadn't truly taken the time to become friends. What would have happened if he had resisted the pull of attraction for Margie, and instead married his friend?

I'm not going there. Water under the bridge, and all that. Deep, muddy, churning water.

Besides, he didn't have the stomach for romance. To use Caleb's terminology, there were still too many ghosts haunting him.

That settled in his mind, he turned back toward the salon. Biting back a sigh, he headed inside, resigned to spending the next few hours reading the boring articles he'd avoided so far. And who knew? Maybe one day he'd be glad he'd found out all about the benefits of mineral-based makeup.

Sigh.

"You are not staying here."

Tired from hours on her feet after four days off, Karina barely had the strength to raise her fork from her plate to her mouth. But she managed a stern expression as she looked across the kitchen table loaded with take-out food.

Mason expertly picked up a piece of broccoli with his chopsticks and held it in front of his mouth before he answered. "I'm not leaving you alone, and that's final. Get over it."

The broccoli went into his mouth. If anyone could chew stubbornly, it was Mason.

Karina set her fork, loaded with a bite of fried rice, on the rim of her plate. "We discussed this last—"

The ringing of his cell phone interrupted her argument. He snatched it up, glanced at the screen and gave her a look before pressing the button to answer.

"Hey, Brent. I wondered what happened to you today." He listened for a second. "Yeah, I tend to forget that some people have real jobs. What did you find out?"

A man's voice sounded through the phone, but since Mason made no move to turn on the speaker, she couldn't make out his words. She picked up her fork and continued to eat while listening to half of the conversation.

"I didn't think so. He's too young to have left much of a trail. But were you able to check his college records, or maybe his law school records?"

Karina looked up from her plate. Law school? They had to be talking about Hector, which meant Mason had asked his friend to investigate Alex's attorney. For some reason that news irritated her. What did he have against the young lawyer? From the very beginning he'd disliked Hector, even before they'd met. He hadn't given him a chance. She arranged her features into a disapproving scowl and aimed it across the table.

Mason ignored her. He shoved the food around on his plate with his chopsticks while listening. "Mm-hm. What about summer jobs?" He fell silent, listening, and his eyes widened. "Really?"

In spite of herself, her interest flared. She leaned forward, straining to distinguish words in the voice she heard.

The smile that widened Mason's lips held a touch of satisfaction. "Well, it's not much. A judge would laugh us out of the courtroom, but it tells me we're on the right track. Thanks, buddy. Talk to you soon."

He disconnected the call, set the phone on the table and returned to his meal without saying anything further.

"Well?" Karina turned the word into a demand.

That got an innocent stare. "Well what?"

Honestly! How could any one man express such concern for her one minute and be so incredibly annoying in the next?

"What did your friend say about Hector?"

"Oh, that." He plucked a piece of beef from his plate. "He doesn't have a record, not even a speeding ticket. Got decent grades in law school, and graduated dead center of his class."

She shook her head, impressed. "How did he find that out?"

"He's a computer genius. Maybe he hacked into the law school's records or something. Anyway, Navarro checked out completely clean."

Leaning back in her chair, she allowed an I-told-you-so smirk. "I'm not at all surprised."

Mason seemed unconcerned. "There's more. The only job Navarro ever had was working for a fast food restaurant during the summers while he was in college. And before you ask, it's a national chain owned by a corporation in Kentucky, and there's no connection to any of Maddox's companies."

His manner was too confident, too smug. There was something else.

"So, what's the connection? What would a judge laugh out of the courtroom?"

The smile he'd been holding back broke forth. "Navarro never worked for Maddox. But his *mother* is a private duty nurse."

"Let me guess. Hector's mother is Mrs. Maddox's nurse."

His smile dimmed. "Well, not anymore. But she used to be, back when Hector was in high school. And even though he passed the bar exam only a few months ago, the only debt Navarro has is a car loan. No school loans. That means his college and law school were paid for. Since we know he wasn't a brainiac, he probably didn't get any scholarships. And since nurses don't make tons of money, I'm betting somebody paid Navarro's way." He leaned forward, across his plate. "Maybe he's working for Maddox out of gratitude for putting him through school."

"Mason, that's crazy." She stared at him. "You're looking for a reason to distrust Hector. As many businesses as Maddox owns, there's bound to be a connection to almost every one in this city if you look hard enough. But that doesn't mean they're all involved in something dishonest."

"I'm being cautious." He tossed the chopsticks onto the table. "Somebody around here has to."

Silence stretched between them. The longer it grew, the more disturbed she became. This wasn't simply caution. This was a grudge. He blamed Maddox for his wife's death, and if he couldn't prove that, he'd find a way to prove him guilty of something else.

Lord, what have I gotten myself into? And more importantly, what have I gotten Alex into?

She scooted her plate to one side and reached across the table to grab his hand. "Mason, listen to me. I appreciate all you're doing. But I think you're grasping at a bunch of loose threads and trying to weave them into a coat. There's just not enough there to do the job."

She expected him to pull away, maybe even become angry. What she didn't expect was for him to turn his hand over and entwine his fingers in hers. Or for her insides to turn somersaults when he did.

"Karina, you called me for help. I came. Why can't you just trust me?"

As she sat there, staring into eyes the color of a New Mexico morning, the answer hit her.

I do trust him. Heaven help me, but I do.

Gently, moving slowly, she extricated her hand from his and leaned back. Without speaking, she let him see the trust in her eyes.

He answered with a satisfied nod.

"But," she said, her voice loud in the tiny kitchen, "you're *still* not spending the night here."

A familiar dimple appeared in one cheek. "Wanna bet?"

* * *

Mason pounded the pillow and shoved it between his head and the rental car's headrest. Stubborn woman. Like he cared what the neighbors thought. Since when had Karina become so…so prudish?

In the quiet that permeated the interior of the car, he admitted to himself that she'd always been conscious of propriety. One time, when they were teenagers, they'd fallen asleep on the porch swing of her father's house. He had awakened with a start at four in the morning when his body hit the concrete. She'd jerked awake and shoved him out of the swing, practically frantic that the neighbors would think he'd spent the night. And her father and brother were right inside the whole time, slumbering in their beds.

"We have a reputation to maintain," she used to insist. "We're Christians. What we do reflects on Jesus."

Mason squirmed in the seat, trying to find a comfortable position. At the time he had agreed with her. But that was a long time ago. Since then he'd done a lot of things that the Lord he used to worship probably didn't approve of. Dumping Karina to marry Margie was one of them.

And later when Margie was dead and he lay awake through long, empty nights, he might have found solace in the Lord he had served.

A familiar feeling nudged at the corner of his mind. A sense that seemed to say *I'm still here, my son*.

But Mason had grown expert at ignoring that feeling. Why should he pay any attention to the God who had failed to protect Margie? Who had let him be blamed, while the real killer walked free? Still walked free, in fact.

He shifted in the seat again and coughed, not because he needed to, but to interrupt the silence in the car. To drown out the feeling, and the invitation he refused to answer.

Outside, the area surrounding his car grew quiet. Not a soul stirred in the apartment complex, at least not where he could see. In the distance he heard a door slam, and from another direction, the thump of the bass from someone's stereo, but nothing moved. The window in Karina's living room went black. She must be heading to bed now.

With a loud sigh Mason settled into the pillow and pulled the thin blanket she'd given him up under his chin. It was going to be a long night.

FIFTEEN

Her cell phone rang while Karina was finishing up a blow dry for a customer. Normally she never answered her phone while she was working, especially when she had an elderly woman in her chair as she did then, because some had little patience for cell phones and considered it rude for their hairdresser to interrupt their visit. But Alex was only allowed phone calls at limited times, and she didn't want to miss a call from him.

Mason had come to work with her this morning, of course. He'd taken on the role of self-appointed bodyguard. She had to admit his presence gave her an unexpected sense of security. Sleep had not eluded her last night as it had the night before, and a big part of the reason was the fact that she knew he was keeping watch right outside her front door. She'd felt guilty for sending him out to sleep in the car. No doubt her neighbors wouldn't even notice, much less care. Though she would never admit it to Mason in a million years, her reason had nothing to do with appearances and everything to do with avoiding temptation. When he'd opened up to her yesterday about his feelings, a hard place inside her had softened. During the long hours of the night after a stressful, frightening day, she was feeling a bit vulnerable. No sense putting either of them in a situation that might lead to something they'd be sorry for. As her pastor was fond of saying, the best way to resist temptation was to avoid it.

At the sound of the ringtone, Mason stopped his pacing and turned toward her.

She flipped off the hair dryer and smiled an apology. "Excuse me, Mrs. Sanders."

"You go ahead." The woman lifted a hand beneath the thin nylon apron and waved an approval. "I'm not in any hurry."

Karina grabbed her phone from the counter and glanced at it. An unfamiliar number appeared on the screen. She caught Mason's eye, her eyebrows arched in a question, and answered the call.

"Hello?"

"Ms. Guerrero? This is Hector Navarro. Could you come down to the juvenile justice center at your earliest convenience?"

"Is everything all right?"

His reply didn't answer the question. "There's been a development in Alexander's case. I spoke with him briefly a few minutes ago, and he became agitated."

Her grip tightened on the phone. "What's happened? What did they say?"

A pause. "They've decided to request that the judge remand Alexander's case to criminal court."

The words seemed to bounce off of her brain without registering. "I'm sorry. Remand to criminal court? What does that mean?"

Hector's voice softened. "They want to try Alexander for first-degree murder as an adult, and seek the maximum penalty."

The room around her careened sideways. Karina staggered backward until she was resting against her station, otherwise she might have fallen on the floor. "No. They can't do that, can they? He's only fourteen. And he didn't kill anybody."

Fear made her voice shrill, and it pierced through the salon. From her station nearby Lana paused with her shears overtop her customer's head and turned to look at her with arched eyebrows. Mrs. Sanders's mouth dropped open. Mason hurried across the room and put a hand beneath her arm for support.

"What's happened?" he asked.

She couldn't answer, could only shake her head as she listened to Hector's voice.

"This is disturbing news, but it's not completely unexpected. I tried to explain that to Alexander, but he became upset."

"I don't blame him. I'm upset, too." She found that she had shouted into the phone. "You might have expected this, but we sure didn't."

"Ms. Guerrero, I understand that you're upset. I'd

like to discuss this with you in person. When can
you get here?"

Her brain felt fuzzy, stuffed full of cotton. She
couldn't think, couldn't grasp this terrible news. Poor
Alex must be frantic, and all by himself. Choking
back a sob, she said, "I'm leaving now. I'll be there
in half an hour."

She disconnected the call with fingers gone numb,
and the phone slipped from her grasp. It crashed to
the floor and the battery skidded across the tile. This
nightmare just got worse and worse. How much more
could she handle without falling apart?

In the next moment strong arms surrounded her.
Mason crushed her to his chest and held her trembling body close.

"I don't know what's happened, but whatever it
is, you're not in this alone. I'm here. We'll deal with
it together."

Mason stood in a corner, his arms folded across
his chest, and glared at the dispassionate public defender. Navarro sat in the same chair he'd occupied
the previous day, the same spiral notebook open before him. At least he wasn't writing everything down
word for word today. But neither did he look directly
into his client's face. Or his client's sister's.

Karina had scooted her chair as close to Alex's as
it would go, and sat with his arm clutched in both
hands. Tears flowed unchecked down her cheeks, and
every now and then she gave a little sniff. But at least

there was no sign of the uncontrollable sobs that had wracked her body during the drive here. Alex, his expression as wooden as a log, stared at the tabletop in front of him and didn't say a word.

"The judge might not grant the request," Navarro said. "It's just the D.A.'s recommendation at this point."

"What do you think he'll do?"

The lawyer considered for a moment, then dipped his head. "I think he'll agree with the D.A."

Because Mason was watching Alex's face, he saw fear flare briefly in the teen's eyes. A second later it was gone, and his expression became stoic once again.

"But why?" Karina asked. "Why would the D.A. want to try Alex as an adult? He's never been in any trouble."

"Youth gang crime has become a huge problem in this country, and Albuquerque is cracking down on gang violence. We're going to see this happen more and more as the justice system sends a strong message to street gangs."

Alex did react then. His head jerked sideways and he leveled a glare on the attorney. "I'm not in any gang, and neither was José."

The man flinched at the force of his words, and even Karina's eyes widened. Mason had seen this kid lie, and he would swear to anyone anywhere that Alex was telling the truth.

To give Navarro credit, his voice inflection didn't

change a bit. He answered in the same calm, dispassionate tone he'd used before. "You've said that, and we will tell that to the judge. But the police report I read says you've been seen with acknowledged gang members, and the district attorney is sure to point that out to the judge. Between that and the drugs found in your system—"

The kid exploded out of his chair. "I don't do drugs, either. Why doesn't anybody believe me?" He leaned forward and pounded a fist on the table. The sound seemed to bounce off the naked walls of the small room.

Navarro did move then. He reared back in his seat and actually looked up at his client. With a big kid like Alex towering over him, an angry flush turning his face purple, Mason could hardly blame the puny little man for looking afraid.

The door opened and the guard rushed into the room. "What's going on in here? Counselor, is everything okay?"

Karina stood, grabbed Alex's arm and pulled him back to his chair.

Navarro clicked his pen closed and shut the cover of the notebook. "Everything's fine. I'm just about finished here." He slid the notebook off the table and stored it in his briefcase. "A hearing's been requested. As soon as I find out when we're on the court's docket, I'll be in touch."

Briefcase in hand, he stood and headed for the door and the safety of the guard.

"Wait!" Karina turned away from Alex, her hand out toward the lawyer. "When can Alex go home? Will the judge give him bail?"

Navarro's gaze flicked to where Alex stood, his hands still formed into fists. "I very much doubt it." With that, he hurried through the doorway.

The guard gestured toward Alex. "Come on, Guerrero. Time to go back."

They'd arrived only ten minutes ago. Mason took a step into the center of the room. "Could we have a little longer? Just a few more minutes, to calm everybody down." He sent a stern glance toward Alex.

The guard hesitated, then nodded. "You've got twenty left." He closed the door behind him and returned to his desk.

Mason approached the table and stood opposite Alex. He looked the kid in the face. "Now, suppose you tell us what's really going on."

Karina drew herself up. "What do you mean? He's told us the truth from the beginning."

Mason answered quietly, without releasing Alex's gaze. "No, he hasn't."

Alex remained silent for a moment. His gaze dropped to the table, and Mason saw his throat move as he swallowed. If he hadn't been watching closely, he might have missed the single, tiny tear that shone in the corner of the teen's eye but then was blinked away. Compassion stirred in Mason. Alex looked like a man, because of his size and the seriousness of his situation. But he was, after all, just a kid. And frightened.

Finally, he looked back up and nodded. "Okay. But you can't tell anyone what I say." He looked at his sister. "Promise?"

She glanced at Mason. "But if it will help your case—"

"Promise! Otherwise I might as well go back to my room now, because I'm not saying anything."

Karina looked at Mason. Her face mirrored his questions, only with more emotions. He lifted his shoulders in a faint shrug. What option did they have? Alex was the only person who knew the whole story.

After a few moments she nodded. "We promise."

The kid's glance slid from Karina to Mason, and then he nodded. "Okay. You'd better sit down."

They each took a chair. Mason sat across the table, so he could watch Alex head-on. He placed his hands on the surface before him and entwined his fingers.

"All right, Alex. Tell us what really happened last Friday night."

SIXTEEN

"It started a few months ago," Alex began, "back at the beginning of the summer. Me and José both had jobs, and we were making some money. Not much, but better than nothing."

If Mason had been a lousy attorney, like Navarro, he would have taken notes. But he'd never been one to rely on notes. He leaned back against the plastic chair and gave Alex his full attention.

"Then one day Mr. Velesquez comes to me and asks do I want to make some extra money running an errand for him." He sat quietly in his chair, facing forward, his hands invisible to Mason beneath the tabletop, but the muscles in his forearms moved, as though his fists were clenching and unclenching beneath the cover of the table. He shrugged. "Well, yeah, sure. I'm all about earning money. So he asks me to take this package over to the Casa del Sol restaurant."

Karina interrupted. "The one where José worked?"

Alex cast a guilty glance sideways, and then nodded. Mason fixed Karina with a stern gaze and tried to send a private message to her. *Don't talk or you might intimidate him. Let him do the talking.* She must have gotten the message, because her lips snapped shut.

"It was a big package, kinda heavy. Woulda been a lot easier for him to drive it over in his van, but he said he couldn't leave the store for a while, and the restaurant needed it. There's eight blocks between the Superette and the restaurant, and by the time I got there, my arms felt like somebody had set them on fire." His right hand massaged his left shoulder in an unconscious gesture.

"Did you know what was in the package?" Mason asked.

Alex shook his head. "Mr. Velesquez told me not to look, so I didn't. I didn't see what was in it, because it was all wrapped up." His gaze dropped to the table, embarrassed. "Yeah, I know. It sounds pretty stupid now. And I admit I worried if it might be something illegal, like maybe drugs or something. But it was so heavy I didn't think so. I figured it must be some sort of grocery thing, you know?"

From the corner of his eye Mason saw Karina sitting on the edge of her chair, her body rigid. He ignored her and nodded at Alex. "Go on."

"It was about that time that Mr. Sastrias paid José to take a package to Powerhouse."

At the name of the fitness center, it took all of Mason's self-control not to leap out of his seat and pace around the room. Alex had only been nine years old when Margie was killed, so he probably didn't know the significance of the place. And it was obvious from the way he casually named the gym and continued with his story that he did not. But beside him Karina's eyes went perfectly round. Forcing himself not to look her way, Mason kept his attention on Alex.

"We went on like that for a few months. A couple of packages a week and I got fifty bucks extra, plus my time on the clock. Sometimes Mr. Velesquez had me run a package over to the gym, but mostly I took mine to the restaurant."

"Were they always the same size?" asked Mason.

Alex shook his head. "Sometimes they were square and small enough to fit inside my backpack. Sometimes long." He shrugged. "It just depended."

"And you never looked inside?" Though Alex's body language told Mason he was being entirely truthful this time, he could hardly believe a four-teen-year-old kid wouldn't be curious enough to peek, at least once.

But Alex shook his head. "I wanted to, but they were always taped up real tight." Spots of color appeared on his cheeks, and his eyes darkened. "But José did. Last Friday he unwrapped one of his pack-ages on his way to the gym. He came over to the Su-perette where I was restocking the back room and showed me. And that's when we knew we were in real trouble."

Though Mason had warned Karina not to speak,

she piped up with a question, her expression betraying her curiosity. "What was in it?"

Alex remained silent a minute, examining his hands in his lap. When he answered, his voice was soft. "It was pieces of a gun. A big gun, like…" He hesitated. "Like an assault rifle. We know, 'cause we looked it up on the internet in the back office."

Silence descended on the room. Mason leaned back in his chair and let Alex's words sink in. Parts of assault rifles being delivered between the Superette, Casa del Sol, and the fitness center where his wife worked when she was murdered.

Somewhere deep inside him a flicker of excitement flared. This was the piece of the puzzle that he'd missed four years ago, when he was trying to prove that Maddox was somehow involved in Margie's death. He'd suspected drugs—it seemed everyone was involved in drugs these days—but he'd been wrong. It was weapons. Illegal weapons.

Alex leaned forward, his face thrust across the table. "José told me, and we talked about it. We were both scared, real scared. Coupla months ago I saw a report on the television news about this border cop who got killed by a drug cartel from down in Mexico, but the gun had been built right here in Albuquerque. And I thought, What if one of those packages I delivered had part of that gun in it? I might be responsible for killing that guy." He looked faintly sick at the idea.

"It wouldn't be your fault." Karina placed a hand on his arm. "You didn't know."

Alex didn't look at her, but held Mason's gaze. And Mason knew what he meant. Of course a sister would say that. But a guy knew the truth. Being a pawn and not questioning was as bad as acting with full knowledge. In some ways it was worse, because who wanted to be a dupe?

Mason nodded. "I understand. So after you and José realized what was happening, what did you do?"

Alex leaned back in his chair. "We decided to quit our jobs. Both of us. I decided to tell Mr. Velesquez I was having trouble at school and my sister was making me stop working." He ducked his head and shifted in the chair so his body was angled away from Karina. "I was afraid to tell him I'd figured out about those packages."

Mason nodded. "That was a smart move."

"Yeah." The teen's shoulders heaved with a silent laugh. "If José had done the same thing, maybe I wouldn't be in this mess. But he couldn't let it lay. Our plan was for him to go ahead and deliver the package to the gym and go back to work. Then both of us were going to quit our jobs when we left work for the night.

"Nothing worked out right, though. Mr. Velesquez had to go to a meeting or something, and he left another guy running the register. So I couldn't quit. And then José messed everything up. Instead of going to the gym, like we'd decided, he took the package he'd opened back to Mr. Sastrias and told him he wouldn't deliver any more for him." Alex slid down in the chair, shaking his head. "Stupid idiot. I wish he hadn't done that."

Mason was developing an image of José in his mind. *Stupid idiot* was probably an apt description, but he couldn't help admiring the kid's moxy. It took a peculiar brand of guts to confront an illegal arms dealer on his own turf. When he'd been fourteen, he certainly hadn't possessed it.

And yet that moxy had been terribly misplaced. It had gotten José killed.

Karina had fallen silent. She watched Alex out of the corner of her eye, but wisely held her tongue. The clock on the wall told him they only had about five more minutes before the guard came to take Alex back to his room.

"What happened Friday night?" he asked.

A miserable expression overtook Alex's features. "I knew Mr. Velesquez was coming back to the store around midnight to close out the week. I arranged to spend the night with José so he could go with me. We waited until his parents went to bed, then slipped out. José waited while I went into the back office and talked to Mr. Velesquez, and told him my story about my grades slipping. But he didn't believe me." He leaned forward and rested his forehead on the edge of the table. "He told me he had already talked to Mr. Sastrias, and he knew what José had said, and he knew we were friends. I couldn't deny it, because there José was, waiting for me out front in the store. And Mr. Velesquez told me that I shouldn't quit, because a smart young man like me could make a lot of money working for his bosses."

He fell silent. Watching him, Mason could see a fierce struggle taking place in the young man's face. Out of the corner of his eye he saw Karina's shoulders rise as she drew breath to speak, but he warned her with a quick glance. The kid needed to work out the memory and tell the tale in his own time.

Seconds ticked away, and Mason fought an urge to remind Alex that their visitation time would soon end. Finally the boy straightened in the chair.

"I caved. I told Mr. Velesquez I'd think about what he said." His hand rose, and fingers raked through his thick, black hair. "I wasn't going to continue delivering packages for him, really. It's just that every argument I had, he came up with an answer. I couldn't think up any more reasons. I'm such a wimp."

"You're not a wimp," Mason assured him. "An older man who had authority over you persuaded you."

"José didn't cave," the boy said, miserably. "When we left the store, I told him what had happened, and he was angry. Said he'd quit his job to do what was right, and I'd let him down. Even though he was right, it made me mad, and we argued. That's when the guy came up to us."

He stopped, closing his eyes as though to shut out the memory of that night.

"The guy?" Mason prompted.

He nodded. "We'd seen him around a lot, just coming inside the store or the restaurant, hanging out. And he was—"

Whatever description the kid had been about to give was chopped off when his mouth snapped shut. Mason saw true fear in his eyes.

"Was he someone working for the 'bosses' Mr. Velesquez mentioned?"

"I...didn't think so at the time, but now I know he was."

Now they were getting somewhere. Mason leaned forward. If Alex had actually talked to Maddox, could pin him with an illegal weapons charge, that would be perfect. "Is he a big guy? Thick head of dark, partially gray hair? Wears a suit most of the time?"

"N...no, not a suit. He wears—" His mouth closed, tightened, and he shook his head. He continued, but Mason made a mental note to come back to the description. "He told José that Mr. Sastrias sent him to talk him into not quitting. *Persuade you to stay,* is how he said it." Alex shuddered. "We were in this alley, with nobody else around, and José got mouthy with him. José always did have a mouth. The next thing I knew, this guy pulled a gun out of his jacket, and I was so scared I could hardly move. But José wouldn't shut up. Kept talking back, saying the guy had better leave us alone or he'd turn him in, send him to jail."

The color had drained from Alex's face, leaving his skin an unhealthy pasty color.

Karina had gone completely still, as though she

were afraid to move lest she break the flow of Alex's words. Mason waited a moment. Through the window behind Alex's head he saw the guard glance at his watch, look up toward the door, and start to rise from his chair. Their visiting time had almost ended, and he wanted to get back to a description of the guy.

"What happened then, Alex?" Mason kept his voice low and soft.

The boy's shoulders trembled with barely suppressed sobs. "He shot José. Right there. Just pulled the trigger, and then José was on the ground, and he couldn't breathe." His eyes, fixed on some faraway sight, flooded with horror. "And the next thing I knew he shoved the gun into my hands and told me to keep my mouth shut, no matter what. That his boss—*our* boss—would make sure everything came out okay as long as I did exactly what they told me to do. And if I didn't—"

The guard opened the door. "It's time, folks."

Mason leaned across the table and whispered urgently. He couldn't let Alex go back until he knew the whole story. "What did he say would happen if you didn't, Alex?"

With a glance at the guard, Alex rose from his chair and angled his back toward the doorway. Beside him Karina did the same. She looked shell-shocked from the story she'd just heard. A similar expression colored Alex's features, and the resemblance between the two of them at the moment was remarkable.

But then a determined look stole over his features.

He leaned over the table toward Mason and whispered, "He said if I don't cooperate and do exactly as they say, my sister will end up the same as José. And this guy, he can do it. You can't let that happen."

With a final, urgent stare, he allowed the guard to escort him from the room.

SEVENTEEN

Neither of them said anything as they collected their keys and left the building. Not until they were alone in the rental car did Mason dare to speak. He started the engine and reversed out of his parking space.

"I'm glad he finally came clean with us," he told Karina.

"I know." She retrieved her purse from the floorboard and pulled out her cell phone. "We'd better let Hector know what Alex got mixed up in."

Mason slammed his foot on the brake pedal, and the car jerked to a halt. "Have you lost your mind?" He reached over and grabbed the phone from her hand.

Anger flared in her face. "He's Alex's lawyer. He needs to know the truth."

Shaking his head, Mason gave her a pitying look. "You are way too trusting, Karina. What's it going to take to convince you that the guy's as crooked as a bent fork?"

"You don't know that," she insisted. "You've decided to dislike him for some reason. I know he doesn't have much experience, but he's all we've got. Maybe if we work *with* him instead of against him, he'll be able to actually do his job."

She had a point. Mason had taken an instant dislike for the weak-kneed lawyer. But something that Alex had said just now had confirmed his suspicions.

"Yesterday did you hear what Navarro said to Alex as he left?"

Karina's face went blank. "That he'd visit with him when he could?"

"No. He said, 'Do exactly as you're told and everything will work out okay.'"

She held up a splayed palm. "So?"

"Didn't you hear your brother just now? That's what the man who shot José said when he shoved the gun into Alex's hands. He said everything would come out okay as long as he does exactly as he's told."

"The same words," she whispered, then nodded. "I remember."

"When he said that yesterday I saw Alex's face. It was like he'd been slapped. Like he'd been sent a message, and he got it."

"So Hector really is working for whoever is responsible for these illegal guns?" Her face went pale. "Alex doesn't have a chance, does he?"

"Well now, I don't know about that." Mason took his foot off the brake pedal and the car rolled forward. "We don't know how high this thing goes. Maybe whoever's in charge has control of the criminal courts, but not the juvenile courts. They might be transferring him in order to make sure they can be assured of the outcome." Mason highly doubted it, but they had to consider all possibilities.

"But what outcome is that? Are they going to have him acquitted and released so he can continue working for them? Or send him to adult prison where he'll be brutalized and…" She slid down in the passenger seat and covered her face with her hands.

While she sobbed quietly, he turned out of the parking lot onto the main road. The details they'd just learned rolled around in his mind, a jumble of facts with very little form. He needed to lay it all out, to talk to someone who could help him make sense of everything. He could arrange a call with Brent and Caleb, his F.A.S.T. partners. This was exactly the kind of thing the three of them were good at, talking things out and making sense where none seemed to exist. But neither of them knew anything about Albuquerque. Plus it was eleven forty-five in Albuquerque, which meant it was one forty-five in Atlanta. Brent was at work, and Mason had bugged him a lot lately. Being a top executive for a giant corporation, he probably couldn't spare an hour or so for a personal meeting until this evening, after he left the office.

There was one person, though, who could help him.

The car glided to a stop at a traffic light, and Mason shifted in his seat to slide his cell phone out of its case on the waistband of his jeans. "I'm going to call Parker. Maybe he can help us make sense of this mess."

He thought Karina might object, but she nodded approval of his plan. Probably too frightened to argue with him. Her eyes were abnormally large, making her look more like a vulnerable little girl than the spitfire woman he knew so well. As he punched in Parker's number, he managed to give her what he hoped was a comforting smile.

Thirty minutes later they were seated in a corner booth with one long curved bench at a busy diner not far from the hair salon. Karina's handbag lay on one end of the bench, which forced her to sit closer to Mason. The opposite bench was left free for Parker. She could have placed the purse between them as a barrier, but she needed the strength of his presence at the moment and the closer the better. Occasionally when he moved, his leg brushed against her and sent a comforting wave through her tense body.

The diner's door opened.

"There he is." Mason's voice held a hint of relief that bothered Karina even more than his usual sarcasm. He must be really worried, which meant her own fears weren't unfounded.

Officer Parker Harding stepped into the diner and held the door open for the person behind him. Another uniformed officer followed him into the restaurant. Karina recognized him as Officer Graham, the other man who'd arrested Alex last Friday night.

"What's he doing here?" Mason asked under his

breath before he stood and caught Parker's attention with a wave.

Officer Graham said something to Parker and then he headed for the restrooms on the opposite side of the diner's long serving counter. Parker came toward them.

Karina remained seated while Mason shook his hand.

"I thought you'd come alone, dude," Mason said as he returned to his seat beside her.

Parker slid onto the bench on the other side of the booth. "I would have, but Grierson has us tied at the hip, especially when it comes to anything about you. I don't think he trusts me." His head turned toward Karina. "How are you doing? Everything okay?"

The sound of his kind tone sparked a prickle of tears behind her eyes. Sarcasm she could take. Kindness, on the other hand, prodded at a tender place deep inside and made her want to weep. She blinked hard, and managed a nod and a half smile. "Last night was better, thank you."

"I kept watch to make sure nobody bothered her place," Mason said.

A chuckle shook Parker's shoulders. "I know. I saw you sleeping in your car."

An outraged expression overtook Mason's features, and he stiffened. "I didn't fall asleep all night."

The chuckle became a laugh. "Dude, you were imitating a chainsaw from around one-thirty until I got off at three."

Karina turned in the seat to give Mason a look. So much for her bodyguard keeping her safe.

He looked a little sheepish, but then rallied in typical Mason fashion. "So I might have drifted off for a few minutes. But if anything had moved, I would have been awake in an instant."

"Right." Parker shook his head. "What I couldn't figure is why you were outside. If anybody broke into that apartment, you'd be able to keep her a lot safer from inside than from a car in the parking lot."

Karina focused on unwrapping her silverware from the paper napkin, aware of Mason's I-told-you-so look beside her.

"Long story." He raised his head, and she followed his gaze to see Officer Graham exit the restroom and begin to thread his way through the tables toward them. "So what about your new partner? Can we trust him?"

Parker half turned to get a look at him. "I think so. He's pretty quiet. Doesn't say much about anything. But he didn't narc us out to Grierson yesterday. He knows when to keep his mouth shut."

His answer didn't have the ring of a wholehearted endorsement, and left Karina a little uneasy. She exchanged a glance with Mason. His shoulder lifted a fraction and he said under his breath to her, "We'll play it by ear." Then Officer Graham arrived, and Parker slid over in the booth to make room for him.

"Ms. Guerrero." He nodded a greeting across the

table to her, and then turned a slightly more guarded gaze on Mason. "Sinclair."

The server arrived with four short glasses of water. When they'd been placed on the table, she picked up her order pad from the round serving tray, held it up to shake off a few drops of water and took their orders. Then she disappeared toward the kitchen.

"On the phone you said you needed help figuring something out." Parker picked up his water glass and held it before his lips. "Has something happened since we talked to you yesterday afternoon?"

Mason shot her a glance with an unspoken question. Should they tell him what they'd discovered? Karina honestly didn't know. If she'd learned anything in the past hour, it was that she'd been absolutely clueless where Alex was concerned. All this time she'd thought she was a good sister, that they had the kind of relationship that her brother would come to her with anything that bothered him. Obviously, she'd been wrong. And then she'd trusted Hector, even though it was beginning to look like Mason was right about him. For some reason she didn't feel comfortable telling these two police officers everything they'd learned, but she didn't trust her own judgment anymore.

Giving a helpless shrug, she nodded for Mason to continue.

"So that's the long and short of it." Mason picked up a French fry from his half-eaten lunch and dunked it in a puddle of ketchup. "We couldn't get anything else out of Alex because we ran out of time."

Parker wiped his mouth with a napkin, wadded it into a ball, and tossed it onto his empty plate. Beside Mason, Karina shoved lettuce around in the salad from which she'd only taken a few bites. Graham had stopped eating halfway through his burger, and leaned back to fix an intent gaze on Mason.

"So Alex didn't identify the man who shot his friend?" Parker lounged back and looked around the booth.

"No, other than to say he didn't fit Maddox's description." Mason washed the fry down with a gulp of lemonade. "But that's not surprising. Somebody like Maddox wouldn't do his own dirty work. He probably has a dozen or more thugs to handle things like snuffing punk kids."

His former partner's lips pressed together into a hard line.

Graham finally ended his silence to ask a question. "Why are you so sure Russell Maddox is involved? Do you have any proof?"

Mason used a French fry as a distraction, chewing while he considered the best way to answer. Something about the way Parker's partner watched him through slightly narrowed eyes, as if he suspected every word he heard, rubbed him the wrong way.

But that's what a good investigator does. He watches. He questions.

Was it possible he was jealous of the guy who was

his former partner's new sidekick? He didn't think so, but he couldn't stop the feeling that the guy was too quiet, too watchful. And apparently Parker wasn't one hundred percent confident in him, either. For that reason alone Mason didn't want to play every card in their hand. It might be best if Graham didn't know he was actively investigating the crime, but thought he was only in town to support his old friends Karina and Alex.

"No physical evidence, if that's what you mean." He glanced over at Parker. "But I've suspected the guy was involved in something shady for a long time."

"Since your wife was murdered, you mean."

Graham's quiet voice drew Mason's gaze back to his face. There he found the first emotion he'd seen in the guy's eyes. Compassion. Mason shifted on the vinyl-covered bench. "Yeah."

Parker stirred the ice in his glass with his straw. "You didn't have any proof then, and you don't have any now. Face it, you're never going to find anything to connect Maddox with Margie's murder."

Mason answered quickly. "I'm not trying to. There's been a new murder, in case you haven't heard." He filled his lungs and blew the breath out. "And even if Maddox isn't involved, the fact that the boys were running packages to the fitness center where she was killed pretty much proves there's a connection between the two deaths."

Both police officers nodded.

"Actually…" Parker exchanged a glance with Graham, who answered with a slow nod. Parker set his glass down on the table and fixed Mason with a direct gaze. "The news of an illegal arms dealer operating in Albuquerque isn't a complete surprise. There's been evidence that something like this was going on for several years. It might even have been in place back when Margie was killed, buddy."

Instead of feeling triumphant, as he could have expected at a confirmation of his suspicions, Mason felt a nearly unbearable sadness. Beneath the cover of the table, Karina slipped a hand inside his. He squeezed it, drawing comfort from the contact.

The server arrived to clear away their empty dishes. An uncomfortable silence fell and continued for a minute or so after she left.

Then Parker leaned across the table, his voice pitched low. "Look, I'll admit something. Ever since you left Albuquerque, I've kept my antennae up for news about Maddox. There's never a hint of suspicion about him. If he's involved in anything illegal, he's so far removed nobody will ever be able to pin it on him."

The news that his old partner had actually listened to his instincts acted like a tonic on Mason. If he could get Parker's help in investigating Maddox, they might actually be able to nail the guy. "But everybody leaves a trail. There's got to be something. What about the crime lab? Have you looked for a connection there?"

Graham bristled at the idea. "That's a ridiculous suggestion. Why would you suspect the crime lab?"

His vehemence rubbed Mason the wrong way. What, did the guy have a buddy in the crime lab or something? He worked hard to control his features as he answered.

"Because Alex insists neither he nor José were using drugs. Or ever used drugs, in fact. So either he's being dishonest, or those lab results were wrong. Either by mistake, or on purpose."

An incredulous expression stole over the guy's face. "And you believe a teenager over professional lab technicians?"

"I do," Karina answered instantly. "My brother doesn't take drugs."

The patronizing smile he turned on her stomped all over Mason's nerves. With an iron will he restrained his tongue, tore his gaze from Graham and looked pointedly at Parker. "There's also the lawyer. Weasel of a guy, so wet behind the ears his collar's probably damp. He used exactly the same phrase in talking to Alex that the killer did. No doubt in my mind at all that he's involved."

"If that's true," insisted Graham, "then you need to contact the D.A."

If that's true? Mason bristled at the implication, but the pressure from Karina's hand on his urged him to silence.

She shook her head. "The district attorney is the

one who is recommending that Alex be tried as an adult. What if he's mixed up with the others?"

Lips pursed, Parker looked at her for a moment, then shook his head. "I can't believe this thing involves lawyers and judges and the crime lab. I mean, look. Illegal dealings are almost a given with all the increase in activity from the Mexican drug cartels in the U.S. lately. We're so close to the border, and we have such a high Hispanic population with ties back to Mexico, we'd be stupid not to suspect some sort of traffic back and forth. Illegal arms?" He shrugged. "I hate to think it's true, but it doesn't really surprise me." He rested his arms on the table and entwined his fingers on the surface. "But I have a hard time accepting a widespread web of crime the size you two are hinting at."

"I don't believe it at all. It's starting to sound like a giant conspiracy theory straight out of Hollywood." Graham slid out of the booth and snatched the check off the table. "I've got this. You guys can handle the tip. I need some air."

He headed for the cash register at the end of the counter without another word.

Mason watched his retreating back. "Nice guy, your new partner. How'd you get stuck with him? Did you lose a bet or something?"

Parker answered with a snort. "Grierson likes him. Told me his focus would balance my tendency to take a scatter-shot approach to investigation." He dug a five out of his wallet and tossed it on the table. Then he slid to the other side of the bench seat so he was look-ing directly across the table into Mason's face. "Look, I hate to say it, but in this case, Graham's right. You sound like one of those conspiracy theorists."

The words acted like water on a fire. Mason's shoulders sagged. "But if Maddox is involved, its gonna be big, right? He's got a finger in every pie in this state." His glance slid to the cash register, where Officer Graham was tucking his change away in his wallet. "Maybe your partner's involved, too. Did you ever think of that?"

The idea startled Parker so much he reared back and flattened his back against the booth's high rear cushion. His mouth opened, and Mason could al-ready hear the protest that was coming. But then he stopped. His eyes unfocused as though something had just occurred to him.

"What is it?" Karina asked.

Parker shook his head and clamped his lips shut. "Nothing. I can't believe that. Graham's like an arrow. He flies the straightest line you ever saw."

If Mason hadn't worked with Parker for over a year back when he first joined the police force, he might not have caught the hint of hesitation in the man's tone. In the next instant, it was gone, and Parker slid out of the booth.

"Gotta go. But listen, I'll keep an ear out. If I hear anything, you'll be the first to know."

Mason stood and shook his hand. "Thanks, buddy. I appreciate it."

The grin returned to Parker's face. "We're on patrol again tonight, so if you feel like taking another nap, go ahead. I'll keep an eye on both of you."

With that jab he sauntered toward the front of the restaurant and disappeared through the door.

Mason returned to his seat. He and Karina sat in silence for a moment. Through the window, they watched the two police cruisers pull out of their parking places and turn onto the road.

"Do you think they're right?" Doubt made Karina's tone heavy. "Are we seeing conspiracies where there aren't any?"

Were they? Mason raised a hand and rubbed it over his velvety soft and freshly clipped hair. The burn on the side of his face stung, a vivid reminder that they weren't simply talking about a hypothetical situation. The danger to Alex and to Karina was real. But from where did it come? How could he fight against an enemy he couldn't see, couldn't identify?

"No." He poured all the confidence he felt into his voice. "They're not right. We're on the right track, I know we are. It's like an upside-down pyramid. Everything balances on that bottom brick. If we can just find some evidence to tie Maddox to these illegal weapons, the whole thing's going to come down into one big pile."

EIGHTEEN

Though she knew Mason didn't want to, Karina insisted on going back to work after lunch. She hated to leave Lana hanging, for one thing. But her main reason was because she didn't know what to do with Mason hovering over her every minute. The brooding silence as he glared at every car that passed had set her nerves on edge and had her jumping at shadows. Even the thought of going back to the apartment and sitting there, watching him pace from the sofa to the window, almost drove her nuts. So she overrode his protests and returned to work for the afternoon. Thankfully the salon was busy for a Thursday, and she was able to ignore her tangled thoughts *and* his brooding, pacing presence.

Night had fallen when they left the shop. They drove through a fast-food restaurant for a supper of hamburgers and fries, and headed for her apartment. When Mason shifted the car into Park, he turned a cautious glance her way.

"So, are you going to make me sleep in the car again tonight?"

Lifting her purse from the floor to sling over her shoulder, she grasped the food bag in her hands and avoided his stare. "Probably."

A grunt sounded loud in the interior of the car. "I figured. Can I at least use your shower first?"

Somewhat relieved that he wasn't putting up an argument, she readily agreed. "Of course. And really, you don't have to stay the night. You could go back to your hotel, or call your friend and use his guest room. I'm sure I'll be fine."

She saw his shoulders heave with a laugh, but before it was fueled by any sound, he froze. The look on his face stirred a tendril of fear deep inside her.

"What is it? What's wrong?"

His head jerked forward, to something beyond the windshield. Karina followed his gaze, and her pulse kicked up speed. Something hung on her front door. Something white and shaped like an envelope.

Reasons fired around in her mind. A shut-off notice, maybe? She'd been late on her electric bill in the past and received the final notice in the form of a letter on her door. But she'd paid her bills this month, all of them. Something about Alex, then?

Without another word, she opened the door and exited the car. As she half ran up the sidewalk to her front door, she was aware that Mason had left the car and was following her. A single sheet of paper without an envelope had been stuck on the front door with a piece of duct tape. From the outside it looked like a sheet of clean everyday typing paper, no writ-

ng visible. She snatched it off the door and flipped
t over to read a hand-lettered note.

*Call off your bloodhound or you'll end up like
his wife.*

The words hit her like blows, and left her mind
inging. Wordlessly she held the paper up for Mason
o see. As he read, color drained from his face.

He took the page from her with a two-fingered
grasp. "We have to show this to Parker."

She wanted to say okay, but for some reason
her throat didn't work. She couldn't force a sound
through. Instead, she nodded. Then she reached into
her purse and grabbed her keys. The door handle,
thank goodness, was still locked.

But the minute she swung the door inward, everything felt different. Strange. Before she even flipped
the light switch, she knew something was wrong.
When she did, she immediately noticed the missing
picture on the living room wall.

Then her gaze dropped to the floor, and her blood
froze in her veins. The family picture of her, Alex
and Papa wasn't missing. There it lay, on the floor,
the glass shattered.

Her shears protruded from the center of Alex's
face.

"Well, whoever this guy is, he doesn't have much
imagination, does he?" Parker stood in a corner be-

side Mason, the two of them watching as Graham used a digital camera to snap pictures of the mess on the floor. "Same message as before."

Mason stared at the shattered frame, at the scissors protruding from the glass. His gaze rose to Karina, who stood in the opposite corner of the small living room, her arms wrapped so tightly around her middle it looked like she might cut off the blood supply to her legs. "He doesn't really need a new method. This one's pretty effective."

Parker cocked his head sideways. "You got a point."

Graham went down on a knee to get a close-up, and spoke as he snapped. "Somebody better call juvy and warn them to put an extra watch on the kid."

Mason didn't like the guy, didn't trust him at all, but he had to admit that was a good idea. At his words, though, Karina started like a scared rabbit. Apparently she hadn't realized this could be as much a threat to Alex as to her.

Her expression became sour. "There was an extra watch on me, wasn't there?" A hand swept toward the mess on the floor. "It didn't seem to do much good."

Beside Mason, Parker shifted on his feet and avoided her fiery gaze. Graham straightened and looked her in the eye. "We weren't watching your house, ma'am. We were watching you."

Before anyone could reply, the front door opened. Not a soft, tentative crack, but a swift swinging of the door inward, as though the person on the other side had turned the knob and given it a kick at the same time. Graham whirled, his hand flying to the weapon holstered on his belt. Beside Mason, Parker actually had his holster strap unsnapped as he took an instinctive step toward Karina.

Mason's pulse reacted as though someone had stomped on the gas pedal and sent his heart into overdrive, but within a couple of heartbeats the tension was past. Detective Grierson stepped into the small living room, a storm gathered on his features.

The man's gaze swept the room, pausing for a moment over the picture frame on the floor and then coming to rest on Mason. A piece of stray glass crunched under his shoes as he stomped over to stand in front of Mason and glare into his face.

"I don't know what's going on here, Sinclair, but one thing's obvious. You're up to your eyeballs in it. And whatever it is stinks."

Four years were stripped away in the span of two seconds, and Mason was once again a suspended police officer standing stiffly at attention while his sergeant practically accused him of murdering his own wife. A hot wave of anger rose from a long-hidden place deep in his soul, where a four-year-old fire smoldered. He stepped forward until the toes of his shoes bumped against Grierson's, and shoved his face until barely an inch of air separated their noses.

"You know what that smell is, Sergeant? It's incompetence, and it stinks."

"The title is *detective*." The words ground out between the man's teeth. "And in about five seconds,

I'm going to slap a pair of cuffs on you and haul you to jail just to get you out of my hair."

They stood so close Mason could count the red lines in Grierson's bloodshot eyes. From behind he felt a steadying hand on his shoulder, heard Parker's whispered, "Back off, buddy. You're not helping."

The words penetrated Mason's red-hot anger. Parker was right. Losing his temper wouldn't solve a thing, and he didn't put it past Grierson to follow through on his threat. Protecting Karina would be impossible from jail. With an effort, he backed up a step and forced a calming breath deep into his lungs.

Grierson's glare didn't soften. He even lifted a hand and pointed a finger directly at Mason's chest. "Stop. Messing. Around. In. My. Case."

The finger stabbed forward with every word, but never made contact with his shirt. A good thing, too, because Mason was doing everything he could to keep his temper in check.

"I'm not doing anything except supporting an old friend during a really tough time." He narrowed his eyelids. "I happen to know what it's like to go through something hard involving someone you love."

Grierson held his gaze for another few seconds, and then turned away without acknowledgment. "What do we have here?"

The question served to release a little of the tension in the room. Mason forced his muscles to relax, and Parker's hand dropped away from his shoulder. Across the room, Karina's chest expanded with a breath, though her arms remained wrapped around her middle.

Graham pointed toward the front door. "Scratches on the deadbolt lock, same as the hairdresser's shop."

"Seems we have someone who's pretty good at picking locks." The detective looked around the room. "Anything else damaged? Anything missing?" The questions were delivered in a softer tone, and he looked toward Karina for the answer.

She shook her head. "I don't think so."

"Those belong to you?" He pointed at the scissors.

"Yes. They were in the bathroom, in a drawer."

"Nothing else missing from that drawer?"

"No. The only other sign that anyone was here is the note."

Grierson's eyebrows arched and his glance transferred to Parker. "Note?"

"Yes, sir." Parker retrieved the zippered evidence bag where he'd put the note when he'd first arrived, and handed it to the detective.

Grierson read it through the plastic, flipped it over to note the blank back side, and handed it back to Parker. Once again, his tone softened when he addressed Karina.

"Looks like somebody doesn't like your friend over there." A jerk of his head indicated Mason. "Maybe it isn't such a good idea to have him around."

Mason bristled, but before he could say anything, Karina replied in an even voice. "My brother and I are all alone, Detective. I don't have anyone else to call. And I don't want to be by myself. I'm afraid."

Her gaze flickered to Mason's briefly, and though her lips didn't form a smile, they softened when she looked at him. That tiny, almost unnoticeable sign set off a tornado in Mason's brain. After all this time and after everything she and Alex had been through, and especially after he had hurt her in the past, she'd come to trust him again.

I can't let her down. Whatever it takes, I'm in this thing till the end.

After a moment, Grierson gave a nod and turned away from Karina. He handed the bagged letter back to Parker. "Harding, get this and that picture frame down to the lab when you finish up here. Maybe they'll find prints on the duct tape. If they do, tell them to cross-check with the hundreds they got off the salon's door this morning. And tell them to rush it." His lips formed a grim line. "They're gonna love that."

"Yes, sir."

Parker took the bag, and Grierson spoke to Graham. "You stay here for the rest of your shift. Park your cruiser right out front. Walk around a little. Make your presence known. If anybody's watching this place, we want them to see that we're looking for them. And stay in touch with Dispatch."

"You want me to come back when I leave the lab?" Parker asked, but Grierson shook his head.

"One officer's all we can spare. You'll have to

cover the rest of yours and Graham's patrol on your own. I don't have the budget to assign anyone for special duty, so we'll have to make do with whoever's already on." He allowed his gaze once again to rest on Mason. "Sinclair, you stay out of my way."

Mason had to grit his teeth to keep from snapping a reply while the detective turned on a heel and marched out of the apartment. The door slammed behind him with even more force than it had opened with.

The room remained silent for a few moments, then Parker slapped Mason on the back. "Well, at least you're making progress. You've got someone to help you keep watch tonight."

Mason made an effort to control his expression. He hadn't trusted Graham this afternoon, and he still didn't. Judging by the suspicious glances Graham kept tossing his way, the feeling was mutual. For all he knew, the officer was on Maddox's payroll along with Navarro. Why would Grierson assign him to guard duty instead of Parker? Was it possible Grierson was in cahoots with Maddox, too?

One thing was certain. Mason wasn't about to entrust Karina's safety to someone even Parker couldn't vouch for one hundred percent. It was time to call in some help from his F.A.S.T. partners.

NINETEEN

Caleb's plane arrived on time at nine twenty-three the next morning. Mason stood beside Karina outside the security gate, yawning as he searched for a glimpse of his friend in the flow of people who exited. It had been another long night, this time spent in the car parked right beside Officer Graham's police cruiser. Mason felt like he needed to watch Graham as much as the apartment. He was slightly comforted that Parker arranged his patrol route that he came by every so often to check on them. Only when the shift changed at four this morning and Graham was replaced by another officer, who seemed to be a decent guy, did Mason allow himself to catch a few hours' sleep.

Spotting Caleb in a crowd wasn't hard. Not only did the guy stand a full head above most everyone else, his looks were distinctive enough to draw attention. Broad shoulders and arms the size of small hams presented an intimidating picture on anyone, but the long hair caught back into a ponytail at the nape of his neck, and the multicolored tattoos that covered both arms, ensured that those who surrounded him gave him plenty of room. Of course if they'd known the gentle giant at all, they wouldn't have been intimidated. Unless, of course, they were freaked out by someone who launched into prayer at the drop of a hat.

"There he is." Mason raised an arm above his head and waved.

Karina's eyes widened. "Wow. He's...big."

"Yeah, don't let his size scare you." He grinned down at her. "You can take him."

Caleb caught sight of them and veered in their direction. When Mason's hand clasped his strong grip, a powerful relief washed over him. Finally someone he could trust to help keep Karina safe.

The big man cocked his head to get a look at the side of Mason's scalp. "Brother, you look like you lost a fight with a blowtorch."

"Yeah. It's nothing." Mason shrugged off his concern. "Listen, thanks for coming on such short notice."

"Not a problem, but do me a favor. Next time you schedule a flight for me, give me more time to change planes. I ran the whole way and even then I almost didn't make the connection."

Mason chuckled at the image of Caleb running through the airport, ponytail flapping in the breeze behind him. People were probably diving sideways to get out of his way.

"Sorry about that, buddy. I wanted you here as soon

as possible." He put a hand at the small of Karina's back. "Karina, this is my friend Caleb Buchannan."

Caleb's giant paw swallowed her dainty hand, and Mason almost laughed at the way she had to tilt her head back to look into his face.

"Thank you for coming on such short notice." Her smile was polite and tentative.

"Happy to do it, Sister. The Lord has sent me out on shorter notice than this. I've learned to be ready to move whenever He does."

The smile transformed itself into a real one. "You're a believer?" Her gaze flicked toward Mason as if shocked that he even knew a Christian.

"Sure am. And Sister, I don't need to see that cross hanging around your neck to know Who you belong to. I can see Him shining in your eyes."

Oh, great. In another minute they'll probably start up a prayer meeting right here in the terminal.

Mason hurried to break into the conversation. "Can we get out of here before you two start singing hymns or something?" He didn't wait for an answer, but headed for the exit.

Karina fell in beside him. Shouldering his duffel bag, Caleb posited himself on her other side. They must have looked like the Mod Squad, pacing through the airport.

In the parking garage Caleb folded himself into the car's backseat. "You couldn't have rented a real car? This one's no bigger than a toy."

From the driver's seat Mason glanced into the

back. Caleb's long legs were scrunched up against the passenger seat, his chin almost resting on his knees.

"Sorry, dude. I didn't know I was going to be chauffeuring a giant around town."

"Oh, here. Let me give you some more leg room." Karina scooted the seat up as far as it would go. "Is that better?"

"I'll be fine, Sister." A chuckle rumbled in the backseat. "I just like to give our friend here a hard time."

"It's a skill he practices," Mason told her as he backed out of the parking space.

It was such a relief to have Caleb here, Mason's mood felt lighter than it had in days. Surely now they'd make some progress. And now that he had help watching out for Karina, he was ready to push the envelope a little.

"Where are we going?" asked Karina as she snapped her seatbelt.

"I think it's time to stop playing around." He turned his head and caught her eye. "Let's see what we can find out from Maddox."

"Are you sure this is a good idea?"

Karina smoothed a crease out of her slacks as she followed Mason out of the elevator on the fifteenth floor of Russell Maddox's office building. If she'd known she would be coming here, she would have taken a little more care with her dress this morning. And her hair was its usual uncontrollable mess. She should have clasped it into submission at the back of her head.

What a dumb thing to worry about it. If we're right, Maddox is a cold-blooded killer who is trying to send my brother to prison. Who cares what he thinks of me?

But the plush carpet of the office, the obviously expensive framed artwork on the walls, the very faint sound of classical music, intimidated her. Not to mention the stylish woman seated behind the gleaming polished wood of the receptionist desk. Makeup perfect, fingernails long and perfectly rounded, shining blond hair caught in an elegant twist at the nape of her neck. The smile she turned on them was cool, professional and not the slightest bit welcoming. She didn't react to the burns on Mason's face at all. Karina didn't attribute the lack of reaction to professionalism—more like she couldn't be bothered to care.

"Welcome to Grayscale Incorporated. How can I help you?"

Karina and Caleb hung back, but not Mason. He marched right up to the edge of the desk and awarded the seated woman a confident smile. "We're here to see Russell Maddox."

"What time is your appointment?"

"We don't have one."

The woman's smile became patronizing. "I'm sorry, but Mr. Maddox is a very busy man."

"I'm sure he is, but we only need a minute of his

time." Mason put a hand on the polished surface of the desk and leaned toward her. "I'm an old friend."

From the stiff arrangement of the woman's features, it was clear she doubted Mason's claim. But his confident manner must have worked, because she said, "Who may I tell him is here?"

"Mason Sinclair. Tell him I'm Margie Sinclair's widower."

For the first time Karina saw emotion flicker on her face. Her eyes softened at the word *widower*. She picked up the telephone, punched two buttons and announced to the person on the other end that a friend of Mr. Maddox's was in the front lobby requesting a few minutes of his time. She gave Mason's name, listened for a moment and then nodded.

When she'd replaced the receiver, she looked back up at Mason. "Please have a seat, Mr. Sinclair. Mr. Maddox's assistant is going to see if he has a moment to speak with you."

Mason turned to award Karina and Caleb a private grin, and gestured toward a small and elegantly appointed waiting area. Karina perched on the edge of a gold upholstered armchair. She barely had time to take in her surroundings before a woman, this one not quite as fashion-model sleek as the first but every bit as professional, approached from around the corner. Steel gray hair cut in a short, sweeping style framed an unsmiling face.

"Mr. Sinclair?"

Mason stepped toward her. "Yes, ma'am."

"Mr. Maddox has a very important conference call in ten minutes, but he'll see you now."

He cocked his head sideways for a second, and then nodded. "Ten minutes should be about right."

No thanks. No apology. In fact, he acted like *he* was the one making time for the meeting, not Maddox. How did he have the nerve to maintain that cocky attitude in the face of such an imposing woman? He held out an arm toward Karina, and she hurried down the hallway after the assistant, a step ahead of Mason and Caleb.

At the end of a long hallway they entered a spacious outer office, apparently the assistant's domain. Standing in the doorway stood the man they had seen leaving Casa del Sol two nights ago.

He came forward, hand extended. "Mason, how are you? It's been a long time. I didn't realize you were back in Albuquerque."

"Just here for a visit," Mason replied as he shook the hand. "Let me introduce my friends, Caleb Buchannan and Karina Guerrero."

Russell Maddox wasn't a small man by any means, but even he had to look up into Caleb's face. For some reason that boosted Karina's confidence and she was able to shake Maddox's hand without trembling.

"A pleasure to meet you both. Please come in." He stepped back and waved them into the office. "Have a seat."

They arranged themselves in comfortable chairs situated in one corner of the office. When Maddox had seated himself, he turned a pleasant expression on Mason.

"So what can I do for you?"

Karina had no idea what Mason planned to say. On the trip over, he would only tell them that he wanted to go straight to the top and see what he could discover by speaking with the "head goon," as he called Maddox. Even so, it came as a shock when he answered with a pleasant smile that was at complete odds with his words.

"We were actually hoping you would call off your goons so Karina's brother could have at least a chance at a fair trial."

Shocked silence rang in the office. With an effort, Karina controlled her urge to gasp. Caleb cleared his throat and gave close attention to the carpet beside his chair. Mason, on the other hand, looked steadily into Maddox's face.

The polite smile slid from the executive's features, leaving a chilly stare in its place. His gaze flickered toward Karina, then back to Mason. "Pardon me?"

"Don't pretend you don't know that Karina's brother is Alexander Guerrero."

She saw understanding dawn in his eyes. "Ah. The young gang member who killed his friend. I did see a report about that on the news."

A flush rose to heat her face, but Karina didn't say anything. This interview was Mason's to handle.

"That's what they're saying. But I think we both know that isn't what happened."

Maddox crossed his legs. "I'm afraid I don't know what you're talking about."

"Oh, come on. We've done our homework. We know you own the grocery store and the restaurant where those boys worked."

A quiet laugh issued from the man, and he folded his arms across his chest. "Not that it makes any difference, but those businesses are owned by subsidiaries, not by me."

Mason continued as though he hadn't spoken. "We also know you've got a couple of lawyers in your pocket." He leaned forward in the chair and rested his forearms on his knees, displaying no sign that he was bluffing. "And we know about the guns."

The man's eyes narrowed to slits. "When your wife was killed, I tolerated your ridiculous accusations because I felt sorry for you. But I'm not as tolerant as I used to be." His gaze flicked toward Caleb. "Nor am I easily intimidated."

"We're not trying to intimidate you." There was not even a hint of a smile on Mason's face now. "But unless you lay off the kid, we're going to take you down. That's a personal promise, from me to you."

The weight of the tension in the room pressed against Karina until she was afraid to breathe, or even move. Finally Maddox got to his feet.

"This interview is over. Joyce?" His call resulted in the door being thrown open immediately and his assistant stepping into the room.

"Yes, sir?"

"Please show Mr. Sinclair and his friends out." He didn't take his gaze off Mason's face. "And then notify security that if they're seen on the premises again, they should be held until the police arrive to arrest them for harassment."

Karina gathered her purse and hurried to the door, Caleb close behind her. Mason took his time, his expression insolent as he passed the woman.

She followed them down the hall and stood watching as they filed onto the elevator. Only when the doors had slid closed and they could no longer see her stern stare did Karina allow her muscles to relax.

Caleb leaned against the back wall and shook his head. "You handled that with your usual finesse, Brother. I'm not sure what you wanted to accomplish, but I don't think you hit your mark."

A satisfied, almost smug expression overtook Mason's features. "Actually, if that guy'd been a target, I just hit the bullseye."

She looked at him. "How so?"

"You didn't see it?" He looked from her to Caleb. "Did you?"

"I didn't see anything except one really ticked off dude who doesn't like you at all."

"What are you talking about, Mason?" Karina asked. "What did you see?"

"I can't believe you didn't see it. Doesn't anybody read body language?"

They both shook their heads.

"When I started talking about Alex, he crossed his

legs. A protective gesture. Then I mentioned the restaurant and store, and he folded his arms."

Karina stared at him, her mind blank. "So?"

"That's another protective gesture, this one stronger. When someone crosses their arms they're creating a shield of protection. But that wasn't the best part."

Caleb watched him, his expression clearly showing he was impressed. "And what was that?"

The elevator stopped, and the doors slid open.

"A tick." Mason grinned at her. "When I said the word *guns,* a muscle below his left eye twitched." He rubbed his hands together like a little boy who'd just been given a birthday present. "We're going to nail this guy."

With that he exited the elevator, leaving them to follow.

TWENTY

The night stretched to unbearable lengths. Mason paced the confines of Karina's small apartment, from the kitchen table where Caleb and she sat to the miniblinds at the front window. Outside a police cruiser was parked again in the first parking space nearest Karina's front door. Not Parker, unfortunately. Once again Grierson had assigned Graham to guard duty and Parker to cover both their patrols.

The conversation in the kitchen had quickly grown uncomfortable. Caleb and Karina had begun by comparing notes on their pastors' preaching styles, and then moved to the controversy over traditional versus contemporary worship music, and had finally settled on their personal beliefs in prayer. That they were both enjoying themselves immensely was obvious from their animation as they talked about their beliefs. Mason had lost interest way back at the beginning and left the table.

He lifted the slats on the blinds and peeked outside. Officer Graham sat in his cruiser, the light from his laptop illuminating his face through the windshield. Mason could just make out the heavy forehead, the square jaw and black caverns where his eyes were located. The head lifted and faced his way, and Mason felt the gaze fix on him. He released the slats and the blinds fell back into place.

Caleb's voice in the kitchen carried into the room. "But I still don't understand how anyone can say 'I Surrender All' isn't every bit as worshipful as one of the more current songs."

"It can be," Karina agreed. "It's all in the delivery style."

It took all Mason's strength not to shout toward the kitchen, *I surrender! If you're going to talk about church all night, just shoot me now and put me out of my misery.*

There had been a time when he could have entered the discussion with a definite opinion. But he hadn't set foot inside a church since Margie's death, and didn't plan to change that any time in the future.

"Amen, Sister." Caleb's voice warmed to his topic. "I wish you could hear the worship team at my church. You'd love them."

The walls of the apartment loomed up on either side of him and seemed to press inward. Next thing he knew, they'd start singing together. If he had to listen to another word about church, screams would be imminent.

His hand was on the door handle almost before he'd made a conscious decision.

"I'm going to take a walk," he shouted into the other room. "Be back in a minute."

"Be careful, Brother. Don't go far."

The words accompanied him as he stepped outside into the night, and then he closed the door behind him. Thank goodness the only things making sounds out here were crickets.

Karina looked toward the kitchen doorway, listening to the sound of the front door closing. Mason had been increasingly agitated as the night progressed. Part of the reason, of course, was the waiting. They'd prodded Russell Maddox, and now they could only wait to see how he'd respond.

But the bigger reason for Mason's irritability was his friend Caleb.

When she was sure Mason had gone outside and couldn't overhear, she lowered her voice and fixed the giant man with a gaze.

"Tell me about Mason these days. He's so different from the man I used to know."

Caleb's gaze followed hers. "He's a hurting soul, Sister. I've known that since I met him a few months after he moved to Atlanta. I could sense the pain in him. I just didn't know how deep his wounds went until your call came on Monday."

"He doesn't go to church at all?"

He shook his head. "Won't even consider coming with me. I've asked several times. But every now and then he says something that shows me he knows more about Scripture than he lets on."

"Oh, he definitely knows his Bible. Or at least he used to." A memory surfaced, and Karina's lips twitched with a smile. "The first year I met Mason, he was the Bible Bingo champion of our youth group. He used to stand up there in the front of the sanctuary and spout verses from memory that I'd never even heard of."

Delight lightened the big man's features. "Bible Bingo champ, huh?"

"Oh, yes. And it wasn't just head knowledge, either." She traced a finger around the rim of the tea mug in front of her. "I once saw him lead three street gang members to the Lord using nothing but Scripture, explained in a way they could understand."

"Mason?" Caleb's stare was incredulous. "The guy who was just here a minute ago?"

She laughed. "The same. Only..." Her laughter faded. "Not the same, either. He's changed."

"His wife's death?" Caleb asked, his voice gentle.

Karina nodded. "I wonder if he blames the Lord for letting her die."

"He wouldn't be the first to question why bad things happen to good people. Or the first to blame God, either." He dipped his head, and forced her to look into his eyes. "How about you, Sister? Are you okay with the bad things in your past?"

The tea had grown cold. She tilted the mug toward her, watched the cool liquid swirl inside. "If you're asking if I've forgiven Mason for dumping me and marrying someone else, then yes. I'm past that."

His next words came as softly as feathers floating on a breeze. "And what about your feelings? Have you been healed of the pain?" His tone dropped to almost a whisper. "Have you gotten over him?"

Regardless of the volume, his question hit her like a slap in the face. Was she over Mason? Could she truly say she had moved on, had put her love for him behind her?

A prickle started behind her eyes, and she couldn't lift her gaze from the cold tea in her mug. "Does anybody ever get over their first love?"

A mitt-sized hand snaked across the table to cover hers. "Not if the Lord gave it to them."

Her vision blurred. "If our love came from the Lord, then why did Mason throw it away for someone else? We shared something precious, and he killed it." She blinked back the tears and rushed on. "I have forgiven him, truly. But I want to know why, especially if…." She didn't finish the sentence, though it burned in her mind. *Especially if I'm going to ever trust in love again.*

His hand pressed on hers. "I wish I knew. But I can tell you that every human being in the world has done something they regret. We've all thrown away the blessings God has in store for us, thinking we were choosing something better. That doesn't mean the blessings stop coming, though. Remember, God is in the business of bringing dead things to life."

She didn't have time to fully consider the meaning behind his words, because at that moment, they heard a shout coming from the vicinity of the front porch.

And then a gunshot.

Mason closed the front door behind him and stood for a moment on the concrete, enjoying the silence. Well, not really *silence*. The neighbors' stereo boomed in the night air, and from one of the apartments on the right a woman's shrill voice was raised in an argument. But it was a comfortable, domestic sort of argument, with no hint of real anger. The kind of argument a mother has with her kids when they ignore her request to brush their teeth and get ready for bed.

A sudden light in the interior of the police cruiser drew his attention. Graham had opened his door, and the dome light illuminated him. Mason eyed the guy. Probably just walking around the area, following Grierson's directions. But no. Instead of turning left or right to pace the sidewalk as he'd done many times the night before, he headed straight for Mason.

Mason narrowed his eyes and watched his approach. What was Graham's role in all this? He was hiding something, of that Mason was sure. Was he in deep with Maddox, or just a paid placement on the force, somebody to keep an eye out on police activity and report back? Or maybe to turn a blind eye at just the right moment, like when a teenager is walking down the street, carrying a heavy package from the Superette to the restaurant?

He arrived at the concrete slab that served as a sort of porch for the first floor apartments in this building, and greeted Mason with a cautious nod.

"Everything all right inside?"

"Just fine." Mason clipped his answer short. He stood with his back to Karina's door, staring out at the parking lot.

Graham stepped up to stand beside him. "You know, your conspiracy theory is pretty hard to believe."

Mason didn't answer. What was this guy up to? A fishing expedition, maybe? The radio clipped to his belt erupted with static and then a female dispatcher's voice called for an officer's ten-twenty. Graham twisted a dial, and the volume decreased as the officer gave his response.

"I mean, the level of corruption you're talking about would have to reach pretty high up in our judicial system. And there'd be cops involved, too. Have to be."

Mason's senses went on full alert. This couldn't be a confession. No reason for the guy to confess to anything, especially to him. There was another reason, and whatever it was, Mason didn't like it.

"Yeah, there would."

"Cops in on an illegal arms scheme." From the corner of his eye, Mason saw him shake his head. "Sits heavy in your gut, doesn't it?"

Mason turned his head a fraction, just enough to get a sideways look at the man's face. The grim lines of his jaw bunched and moved as he ground his teeth. Something was about to happen, something big. Had Maddox sent his pet cop here with a warning? Or maybe with something stronger than a warning? He tensed his muscles, ready to tackle Graham if he even *looked* like he was making a move toward his weapon.

"As I said, hard to believe. I wish I could say impossible to believe." He turned to look Mason in the face. "But I can't."

Here it comes. Mason edged around to face his attacker, and planted his feet squarely on the concrete. *Face an attack head-on. Never let them hit you from the side.*

"What are you trying to say, Graham?"

"I've been nosing around in your record."

Mason blinked. Where was he going with that? "Yeah?"

"You were clean. A solid record. No reason to think you killed your wife. No evidence at all, just that life insurance policy."

That came close to crossing a line. To have a crooked cop bring up Margie's death stirred a deep, smoldering fire and brought Mason's anger to a simmer. His hands tightened into fists. "If you have a point, you'd better get to it."

Their eyes locked in an unbreakable stare. Mason couldn't have torn away if he'd wanted to. But he didn't want to, because he could see secrets hovering in the depths of Graham's intense gaze, secrets... and questions.

And then Graham broke their stare. His eyes moved as his gaze flickered sideways. Surprise registered, and several things happened at once.

The bushes behind Mason's back rustled.

Graham's right hand went toward his holster. He shouted something right in Mason's ear. His left shot out toward Mason.

Instinct kicked in, and Mason ducked and dodged sideways. His next move would have been to ram his head into Graham's gut to throw him off balance. But the chance did not come.

A gunshot cut through the night. The echo rang off the brick building.

The force of the bullet threw Graham backward and he landed on the concrete with a sickening thud.

TWENTY-ONE

His heartbeat pounding in his ears, Mason whirled. Not a soul in sight. Shrubs lined the side of the building on the far end, swallowed by darkness just past the ring of light cast from the bare bulb beside the last apartment door. Should he give chase?

A gurgling sound behind him. He whirled. Dropped to his knees beside Graham. Pressed his ear to the man's nose. There! A faint breath.

"Help!" His shout pierced the night almost as loudly as the gunshot had a few seconds before.

Doors flew open. The one next door, and then two doors down and then, thankfully, Karina's.

"Call 911," he yelled at Caleb. The big man's eyes took in the scene at a glance, and he dashed back into the house.

As Karina rushed forward, Mason remembered Graham's radio. He grabbed the shoulder mic, pressed the button and shouted to the dispatcher. "Ten thirty-three at—" What was Karina's address? His mind grasped and dug up a fact he barely remembered that he knew. "—at Mountain View Apartments on North

Chico. I need an ambulance, and I need it yesterday. Officer down." His throat caught on the words. "I repeat—officer down."

A small crowd had gathered around them. In the distance he heard a siren begin, and then another. His call had been heard.

He jerked his head upward to look toward the corner of the building. The shooter was getting away. He had to go after him.

The dispatcher said something in response to his call, but Mason wasn't listening. Graham gurgled once more, and then went silent.

No! He stopped breathing.

His gaze darted around the circle of observers. "Does anybody here know CPR?"

Nobody answered. Karina dropped to her knees beside him. "I don't, but tell me what to do."

Mason shook his head. It would take longer to tell her how to do it than to do it himself, and time was something Graham didn't have. "No time."

Moving by instincts he thought he'd forgotten long ago, he jerked Graham's body straight. When he did, he felt the hard surface of the trauma plate of a bullet-proof vest beneath his uniform. No way to get effective compressions with that thing on. He was ripping the buttons off his uniform shirt when Caleb reappeared in the doorway, a cell phone held to his ear.

"What's the address here?" he asked.

Four people in the crowd shouted answers. Mason ignored them and continued with his job of exposing

Graham's chest. He was vaguely aware that Caleb relayed the address into the phone. A useless effort, he wanted to say. Help was already on the way. Couldn't they hear the sirens approaching? A whole chorus of them filled the air, coming from all directions.

He ripped the Velcro straps open and jerked the vest away, experiencing another burst of grief. The vest could have saved Graham if the shooter hadn't aimed at his head. "Quiet!" he yelled at the onlookers, and lay his ear on Graham's chest.

Please, please. Let me hear something.

Not a prayer, exactly, because he'd learned long ago that prayers for shooting victims went unanswered. More like a fervent, desperate wish.

A wish that was not granted.

"No heartbeat."

Karina sobbed beside him as he felt for the man's sternum. He rose up on his knees, locked his fingers and placed the heel of his lower hand in exactly the place he'd learned. Then with his elbows locked, he pushed down. Again. Again. Again. At the count of thirty he side-crawled to Graham's head and lifted his chin. He saw the damage now. The bullet had taken him in the cheek. Judging by the amount of blood it had probably hit something vital, but he had to try. He wiped away as much blood as he could, covered his nose and lowered his mouth over the dead officer's. Blew. A deep breath. A wave of relief swept over him when, out of the corner of his eye, he saw the chest rise. That meant, incredibly, the air passage was clear.

Two breaths, and then back to the chest. Pump. Pump. Pump. Thirty times. Now two more breaths.

But as he lowered his head to Graham's, someone rushed up from the side. And then someone else.

"I've got this, sir."

He looked up, and realized the woman talking to him was a paramedic. Red lights flashed in the darkness, throwing spots of color onto the brick apartment building. And blue lights, too. A police car arrived, and an officer jumped out, ran toward him. Then another and another. The parking lot was alive with color.

He shifted away to let the paramedic take his place, and then another one, a man, pushed him away—not unkindly, but firmly—and lowered his ear to Graham's chest. "Bring the shock box," he shouted toward a third paramedic who was rounding the ambulance, then nodded at the woman. She gave the dying officer two breaths, and then the man started compressions.

Mason climbed to his feet and stood over them, watching. A soft arm looped through his, and Karina pulled him gently backward, out of the way. Police officers ran up from all directions, their expressions as they saw one of their own prone on the ground ranging from nausea to fury.

Mason jerked upright. How long had it been? The killer was getting away.

"The shot came from over there." With a jerky motion he pointed toward the corner of the building. "The shooter can't have gotten far."

Three officers nodded, drew their guns and took off. Two others started pushing back the crowd, which was increasing in number by the second. Mason watched, his stomach churning, while the third paramedic ran up with a defibrillator, and the other two stopped CPR long enough to get the paddles in place.

An officer burst through the crowd and ran toward him, his expression frantic.

Parker.

He looked down at his partner's body, and then choked back something that was either a sob or a shout. Then he caught sight of Mason, and rushed over to him.

"What happened?" His hands grabbed Mason's arms and tightened, as if he could squeeze the answer out of him. "Who shot him?"

Words stuck in Mason's throat. He shook his head, and managed to choke. "I don't know. My back was turned. He…"

His voice caught. Caleb placed a huge, steadying hand on his shoulder. Those final seconds replayed in his mind. Graham's gaze sliding from his to something behind him. His hand going toward his gun. Left arm rising, extending toward Mason.

Not to hit him.

Mason closed his eyes, the memory alive. If Gra-

am had been planning to hit him, he would have
ocked his right arm back. Instead, his left arm
eached toward Mason at an angle. He wasn't get-
ing ready to strike. He was trying to shove him out
f the way.

An electrical whine came from the defib ma-
hine, increasing in volume and pitch until the hair
n Mason's arms rose. Then the paddles went onto
Graham's exposed chest, and a *kathunk!* sounded.

The female paramedic placed a stethoscope on his
hest, listened, then shook her head.

"Again," said the first.

Another whine. Another *kathunk*.

Nothing.

Mason closed his eyes, unable to watch anymore.

She had never felt more helpless in her life. Kar-
na stood in the doorway of the kitchen and listened
o Detective Grierson's angry voice. Mason sat in
he living room in the corner chair, his arms on his
highs, his head drooped between hunched shoul-
ers. On the couch, Parker sat with his elbow on the
added arm, his hand covering his eyes, fingers mas-
aging his temple. She wanted to rinse the washcloth
hat lay on the carpet at Mason's feet, the one he'd
sed to wipe Officer Graham's blood from his face.
3ut she didn't dare enter the room.

Behind her Caleb sat at her kitchen table, his lips
noving in a silent prayer. That's what she should be
.oing, too. Praying for Officer Graham's family. He

had a wife, now a widow. Two children who were now fatherless. Pain twisted her heart. She knew the agony of losing a father.

Grierson's shout filled the tiny living room with fury. "I don't know what's going on here, Sinclair, but you'd better start giving me some answers."

Mason shook his head. "I don't know anymore."

"That's not good enough!"

Mason's head jerked up and he fixed Grierson with an angry stare. "Do you think I wouldn't tell you what I knew?" His volume matched the detective's. "A man just died trying to save my life. A police officer is dead because of me. I'm not holding anything back."

Parker unshielded his eyes to scrub his hand across his mouth. "Let's try to stay calm here. Mason, are you sure you didn't see anything?"

Though he continued to glare for a minute at Grierson, he finally heaved a breath and turned a calmer look on Parker. "I wish I had. I heard the bushes rustle. Graham looked at something behind me, and he yelled in my ear. I dodged sideways, and the next thing I knew…"

Karina shut her eyes at the pain on Mason's face.

Father, comfort him. He doesn't know it, but he needs You.

"What were you talking about?" Parker asked.

"Uh." Mason rubbed at his forehead. "We were talking about Maddox, and—"

"Russell Maddox?" Grierson stomped across the carpet to stand in front of Mason. "What about him?"

Mason's gaze connected with Karina's across the room. She didn't think he'd intended to mention Maddox in front of his former boss. The day's stress had caught up with him. He looked tired. And no wonder. For a moment he stiffened, and she thought he might avoid answering. But then his shoulders drooped again.

"I've been doing some checking into the restaurant where José Garcia worked—"

"I knew it." Grierson tossed his hands in the air and whirled around. "I told you to stay out of this investigation, but you wouldn't listen. And now look what's happened. A man's down, a good man. I ought to haul you downtown tonight, you and her," he jerked his head toward Karina, "and that bouncer you've got in the kitchen."

Karina glanced behind her, and Caleb had straightened in his chair. He cast an offended look toward the living room.

Grierson shook his head and heaved a sigh. "But right now I've got to go tell Graham's wife that she gets to raise those kids by herself." He looked at Parker. "And since you were his partner, you get to go with me."

Mason straightened. Every muscle in his body displayed reluctance. "If you want, I'll go, too."

The detective shook a finger in his face. "Not a chance. You are going to stay here and write a detailed statement telling me everything—*everything*—you've done since the minute you stepped off that plane. I want to know every person you've talked to, every place you've been, even every piece of food you've put in your mouth. And I want it in my hand by eight o'clock in the morning. You got that?"

Mason's answer told Karina just how much Officer Graham's death had shaken him. In a meek voice he said, "Yes, sir."

The response surprised Grierson as much as her. His brows arched, and for a moment he said nothing. Then he turned to Parker. "Harding, let's go. I'll leave my car here and ride with you. We have to pick up the grief counselor on the way."

Parker rose. He skirted the coffee table and placed a hand on Mason's slumped shoulder. "I'll talk to you later, buddy."

Behind Karina, Caleb rose from the table and joined her as Parker exited through the front door. Grierson stared at him for a moment, his eyes narrowing to slits.

"I don't know who you are, or why you're here, but see if you can keep him out of trouble, okay?"

Caleb nodded. "I'll do what I can."

The detective's gaze slid to her, and his seemed to soften a bit. But the next instant she thought she was mistaken, because he didn't say anything. Instead he headed toward the door after Parker.

Just before he closed it, he paused and turned to look back into the room. "Sinclair."

Mason looked up.

"It might be a good idea if you three didn't stay

here tonight. Go to a hotel somewhere, one where the rooms open into a hallway, not outside. Ask for an upper floor, so the windows are secure."

Without waiting for an answer, he left. The three of them stared at the closed door in silence.

Finally Caleb said, "I could be wrong, but I think that man knows more than he's letting on."

Karina agreed. And if that were true, then there would only be one reason for his advice to get out of the apartment tonight. If they stayed here, they would be in danger.

TWENTY-TWO

Mason tossed Karina's overnight bag beside his and Caleb's in the trunk of the rental, and climbed into the driver's seat. "How about the Marriott on San Francisco Road? It's got at least ten or twelve floors, and we could get two adjoining rooms." He glared sideways at Karina. "And we're leaving the connecting door open."

He expected an argument in response, but she merely nodded. In the dark interior of the car her eyes were lost in pools of shadow, and her face looked abnormally pale.

No wonder. I'll bet we all look a little shell-shocked.

Mason started the engine and steered out of the parking lot. The clock on the dashboard read almost one in the morning. He kept an eye on the rearview mirror, watching for anything that might look like a tail. Not much traffic in the area right around the apartment complex, so he was fairly confident they weren't being followed.

His gaze connected with Caleb's in the mirror. The big man's chin jerked upward. "You doing okay?"

Referring to the shooting, of course. The sight of Graham's body flooded his mind's eye. A shudder threatened, but Mason controlled it before it took hold. At the moment he wasn't sure he'd ever be okay again.

"Yeah. I'm fine."

Karina twisted around in the seat, one hand holding on to the shoulder strap of the seatbelt. "What were you and Officer Graham talking about when…" She cleared her throat.

"When he shoved me out of the way and took a bullet for me?" He winced at the harsh sound of his voice in the car's otherwise quiet interior. "We were talking about—"

He'd been about to say they were talking about Maddox like he told Grierson, but they weren't. Not really. Mason had been thinking about Maddox. He ran over the conversation in his mind. Maddox's name was never mentioned.

"We were talking about the possibility of an illegal arms racket in Albuquerque, and Graham said he thought there might be something to it." He lifted a shoulder. "Or, actually, he said it wasn't impossible to believe, but a scheme like that would have to be huge to reach all the way up into the court system. And then he kind of changed the subject. Said he'd checked out my record, and it was clean. That he didn't believe I killed Margie."

He fell silent. The mention of Margie brought a wave of grief, as it always did. Only it was even heavier now. Maybe because someone had just died

in front of him, killed the same way she had been
Or maybe it was because of the neighborhood h
steered the car through. They'd lived not far fron
here, in a tiny apartment on the top floor of an ol
house. Quirky, she'd called it. A faint smile tugged a
the corners of his mouth. They could have afforde
something bigger, but Margie didn't want to live ir
a housing development. She wanted to be in a neigh
borhood. And the apartment was close to the fitnes
center where she worked.

With a start, Mason realized the fitness cente
was only a couple of streets away. The place wher
José regularly delivered packages containing weapor
parts. The place where Margie had been gunnee
down while leaving work. Somehow that fitness cen
ter tied the past and the present together.

He glanced in the rearview mirror. Nobody behin
him. Without signaling, he jerked the wheel to th
right and turned onto a side street.

Karina was thrown sideways in her seat. Clutch
ing at the strap, she gave him a startled look. "Wher
are you going?"

"Just humor me for a minute."

Suspicion drew her features together. "You'r
going to that gym, aren't you?"

He didn't answer, but executed another turn.

Caleb spoke up from the back seat. "If I can weig'
in on—"

Mason cut him off. "You can't."

"Why did you bring me here if you're not going t

at least listen to what I have to say?" He turned his head to stare through the window, sulking.

Karina cocked her head. "Gee, where have I heard that before?"

Mason ignored them both. The fitness center lay ahead of them. A sprawling one-story structure with a parking lot in the front and a drive that led around the back. When Mason and Karina had been teenagers, the building had housed a small grocery store. It had closed down during their senior year in high school and had been converted a few years later.

Mason slowed the car near the entrance to the parking lot. His eyes sought out one particular square on the sidewalk, exactly eleven feet from the place where the road concrete changed to asphalt. There. Right there. The muscles in his throat tightened. That's where his wife had died. She'd just left work and was walking toward their home.

Karina's hand snaked across the console. Her fingers touched his arm. No words of sympathy, but he didn't need any. He'd heard them all before. They didn't help.

He jerked the wheel and stepped on the gas. The car bounced as it crossed into the empty parking lot.

"There's nobody here," Caleb commented.

"No kidding?" Mason couldn't have filtered the sarcasm out of his voice if he'd tried. His emotions were too raw, too close to the surface. "I was *sure* we'd find at least a half-dozen gym rats working out at one in the morning."

He rolled through the parking lot, scanning the windows all along the front of the building. They'd been lined with a reflective coating that blocked the sun's rays and made it impossible to see inside. Both Karina and Caleb held their tongues as the car rolled past, and Mason stared at their reflection in the glass. At the end of the building he turned onto the side driveway and headed for the back.

"What are you looking for?" Caleb asked.

The truth was, he had no idea. Something to prove his gut feeling about Maddox was correct? But even if they found proof that the fitness center was involved with illegal arms traffic, Maddox had placed enough padding between himself and this place that nobody would ever be able to get to him.

"I'll know it when I see it," he answered.

The drive opened onto a narrow rear lot. A big loading dock lay at the far end of the building. The huge metal door had rusted, and looked as though it hadn't been opened in years. Beside it, nearer, was a regular door, also of thick metal. A Dumpster sat in the far corner of the lot. Old scraggly trees reached into the sky along the back of the asphalt, and giant scrub bushes had grown up between them to form a barrier to the buildings that lay on the other side. Nothing moved. The place was as deserted in the back as it had looked from the front.

Mason executed a U-turn so the car faced the only exit—a habit he'd learned at the police academy and had never given up—rolled to a stop by the door and shifted into Park. The hum of the idling engine provided a faint background that only made the silence in the car louder.

"I wish we could get inside," he said.

"And see what?" Karina ducked her head to see across him, through the window. "Gym equipment?"

Mason shook his head. "I don't know. Maybe that's all there is. Maybe not."

He noticed something then. Beside the door, mounted on the brick, was a keypad. The kind alarm companies installed in commercial buildings. It looked old, but the buttons glowed with a faint light. Maybe it still worked. Maybe this was the way the manager got inside every morning.

He opened the door and got out.

"Hey, Brother, where are you going?"

Caleb's voice called after him, but he ignored it. He approached the keypad, bent over to examine it. The numbers on the buttons were almost rubbed off from frequent use.

Two car doors slammed, and then Karina and Caleb were beside him.

"This thing looks like it's still being used," he commented.

Caleb looked at it, then into his face. "Yeah. So?"

"So, I wonder if we can get in."

Karina's eyes widened. "Mason, you can't be serious."

"Oh yeah. I can be. And I am." He looked from her to Caleb and back again. "Don't you two see? There's something going on. Graham knew what it was, or at least he suspected. Grierson knows something. I'll bet if we can get inside we'll find something in the manager's office. Some sort of documentation or something that we can use as proof."

"Proof of what?" Caleb asked. "Brother, that man we talked to today isn't dumb enough to leave written records lying around that will point to him."

Mason held Karina's gaze when he answered. "Maybe you're right. But maybe we'll find proof that Alex didn't kill José. Or at least something that will leave a questionable doubt in the minds of a jury."

Her lips twisted as she thought about that. Then she nodded. "If we can do that, Alex will be found not guilty."

"Exactly."

Caleb's head was still shaking. "I don't like it. Besides, how are you going to get in there?" He tapped on the keypad. "This means there's an alarm system. Unless you have skills I don't know about, we can't crack an alarm code."

Mason clamped his jaw shut. Therein lay the problem. He could barely manage to remember the code to the alarm in his home, much less figure out someone else's.

But he knew someone who might be able to.

He grinned at Caleb. "It's for times like these we have a computer geek at our beck and call, right?"

He whipped out his cell phone and dialed Brent's number. The line rang four times, and then went to voice mail. Mason immediately dialed again. This time the call was answered on the second ring.

Brent's voice, husky with sleep, came on the line. "Are you *seriously* calling me at three fifteen in the morning?"

Mason had forgotten the time difference between Albuquerque and Atlanta. But even if he'd remembered, that wouldn't have made a difference. He ignored the cranky comment.

"Power up your computer, dude. I need you to work some techno-magic and get me past a security system."

In the background he heard a sleepy woman's voice ask a question. Lauren, Brent's wife.

"It's Mason," Brent answered. "Who else would have the nerve?" Then into the phone. "Where are you, anyway?"

Mason examined the darkness around him. "I'm standing in a parking lot, trying to get into the fitness center where my wife worked when she was murdered."

A pause. He heard the shuffling sounds of movement, and knew Brent had gotten out of bed.

"All right, give me a minute to boot up. Did Caleb arrive okay this morning? I haven't heard anything from either of you all day."

"Yeah, he's here. We've had a bit of excitement tonight. I'll tell you about it later."

The time seemed to stretch into hours. Familiar computer tones sounded in the background. A minute or so later Brent said, "Okay, I'm ready. What kind of system is it?"

The company name was etched on the side of the keypad. "Sugarcreek Security Systems."

"Sugarcreek." Computer keys tapped in the background. "Yeah, here it is. Hmm. I wonder what kind of system it is."

He examined the keypad, but couldn't find a model number. Of course, that didn't mean a thing. This was just the access panel. The real system lay inside somewhere, probably in the back office. "It looks pretty old."

"Well, let's hope not. It's going to be hard to disrupt the code in an old analog system. But if it's a voice-over IP system with a digital signal, I might be able to do something. Give me a minute."

Minutes passed, during which the only sound Mason could hear was the tapping of keys and Brent's breath coming in over the phone.

"Let me see. Looks like you're at 756 West Jefferson Avenue?"

Mason held the phone out and looked at it. Amazing. He'd known there was a GPS system in this fancy device, but had no idea it could pinpoint his location down to a specific street address. Karina and Caleb both watched him, unspoken questions etched on their faces. Mason shook his head and put the phone back to his ear.

"Yeah, that's right."

"Okay, I'm tapping into you now and scanning for

signals in your area. Stand as close to the alarm system as you can."

Mason edged toward the wall and bent at the waist until his cell phone, still held to his ear, was inches away from the keypad. "I'm right next to it."

"Good. Give me a minute."

More tapping, and then a long pause.

And then a sound that cracked almost as loud as a gunshot in the parking lot. The click of a door lock.

Mason grabbed the metal handle and shoved it downward. All the way down. He could hardly believe it. Karina's mouth hung open, and Caleb's eyeballs nearly popped out of his head.

"We're in." He pulled the door open, speaking into the phone at the same time. "Dude, you rock."

A smile sounded in Brent's response. "Next time give me something hard." His tone became serious. "I assume you know what you're doing, right?"

"Yeah, yeah," Mason replied. "Don't worry. I can handle it. Go back to bed."

He disconnected the call and pulled the door open. Exchanging a glance with Caleb, he stepped forward. The big man nodded and stepped in front of Karina. He put a protective arm in front of her, and followed Mason across the threshold.

Inside the fitness center, nothing moved. Mason stood, statuelike, and scanned the room. The shadowy, spidery figures of exercise equipment filled a wide-open area. Beneath his shoes the same thin, worn carpet he remembered. The combined odors of stale sweat and antiseptic spray filled his nostrils.

The door started to swing closed behind Karina, but in the moment before it latched shut, he leaped backward and caught it.

"We might trigger the alarm if we open it when we leave."

He found that he had whispered the explanation, though he couldn't say for sure why. Obviously no one could hear. He looked around for something to wedge in the door, but came up empty.

"Here." Karina slipped off a sandal and offered it to him. "I'll get it on the way out."

He set the thin shoe in the crack between the door and the doorjamb while she removed the other one and set it aside. Then they crept forward.

The office was in the corner to their right, and he directed Caleb there with a nod. The door was closed, but when Caleb turned the knob, it opened. He grinned at Mason, opened the door and went inside.

"Help him check the files," Mason told Karina. "I'm going to look around out here."

A look of understanding dawned in her face. Once more, she placed a hand on his arm. At the touch of her soft skin, a wave of sorrow nearly overpowered him, and he realized how close to the surface his emotions were in this place where Margie had worked. Had spent her last hours on this earth. Wordlessly, he covered Karina's hand, and smiled his appreciation for the comfort she offered. Then she left him to join Caleb in the office.

Mason stepped into the workout area. Exercise machines surrounded him. He had avoided gyms since Margie's death, finding them too painful. The equipment looked different than when he'd been here last. Sleeker. Newer. Not as clunky as the old stuff. The free weights in the far corner looked the same, in fact that steel rack was probably the same one he'd used four years ago. The rest of the equipment had been replaced, though. Except...

His gaze fell on an old machine tucked off to the right. An abduction machine, with a black vinyl seat, knee pads and a metal peg that could be moved downward to increase the resistance. A sign hung on the stack of weights. *Out of Order*.

Mason couldn't stop a smile. That machine had been out of order back when he worked out here. Funny they'd never repaired it.

The smile melted off of his face. Not just funny. Strange. Unusually so. He studied the rest of the equipment. New, all of it. All except that one machine.

He crossed the floor, his shoes silent on the thin carpet, and stood before the machine. The curly vinyl-covered wire that held the pin in place dangled from the top weight, broken. A hole in the bracket on the left side of the frame was empty, missing the bolt that would hold the moving arm in place. The exact same malfunction as four years ago.

Mason circled the machine, examining it from every angle. Why had management replaced every piece of equipment in the place except this one? And if they weren't going to replace it, why not at least repair it?

That was when he noticed the carpet. There was almost no nap left on any of it, so if he hadn't been studying the machine closely he would have missed the indention. But once he looked, the evidence was unmistakable. The carpet held the faint, almost imperceptible, outline of the machine just beside its current position.

He lifted his face toward the office. "Caleb!" His stage whisper produced no response. He spoke in a normal voice. "Caleb! Come here."

The big man appeared, Karina at his heels.

"We haven't found anything yet," he said as he crossed the floor to join Mason.

"Well, I might have. Give me a hand moving this."

Mason went to the back of the equipment, and jerked his head toward the front. They grappled for a moment to find a handhold, and then bent their knees.

"One. Two." Mason counted off, and braced himself. "Three."

They lifted together. The thing was heavy, which, of course, it would be with a stack of weights on it. Together they barely managed to lift it an inch off the carpet, and then move it quickly to the side.

When they'd set it down, Mason gazed in triumph at the place they'd just uncovered. Beneath the abduction machine lay a carpeted panel. He lifted it and uncovered an indented area in the flooring. Inside, about eight inches down, was a lever.

This was it! His insides jumped with an excitement he could barely control. They'd found something. Whatever it was would surely, *surely,* help them prove Alex's innocence, and maybe even lead them to Margie's killer.

He knelt down and grasped the metal bar. His gaze sought Karina's.

"Should I?"

Grinning with almost as much excitement as he felt, she nodded. When their eyes met he felt a jolt of energy arc between them. He was living in the moment, even as he unearthed the ghosts of his past, with Karina beside him. And it felt right.

TWENTY-THREE

It was like something out of a science fiction movie. Karina watched Mason fidget with the lever for a moment. Finally he pulled it straight up.

The floor-to-ceiling mirror in front of her moved.

Beside her Caleb gave a low whistle. "Would you look at that?"

The middle panel of the mirror receded inward, and then, with a screech of gears that cried for oil, slid to one side. In the gap left by the open panel, a narrow staircase led downward into darkness.

Mason and Caleb straightened, and the three of them stood still for a moment, staring. Karina strained to see down the stairs, but the dim light from the streetlights outside only illuminated the first two steps. The rest disappeared into blackness.

She shook herself to get rid of any creepy ideas. She knew exactly where that stairway led. The old grocery store probably had a basement. And if she were to bet, she'd say the basement had been converted into storage space for illegal weapons.

Mason's gaze caught hers. A fierce satisfaction gleamed in his eyes. "Wanna check it out?"

"Now, Brother." Beside her Caleb shook his head, a scowl gathered on his forehead. "Don't you think we should call somebody before we go investigating dark cellars?"

"And tell them what? That we found a stairway behind a mirror?" Mason snorted at the idea. He started forward. "Just a quick peek, and then we'll make a call."

Karina was torn. Her instincts told her Caleb was right. They should call someone before they descended those stairs. But Mason was already on his way down. With a helpless glance toward Caleb, whose scowl could have boiled ice cubes, she followed Mason.

The stairs were made of wooden slats, worn soft from decades of footsteps. The dank smell of old, wet concrete rose from the darkness when Karina approached, her hand on Mason's back for comfort. He flipped a switch in the wall at the top, and below an ancient fluorescent light flickered on. It shed a dim white light over the basement. At the bottom of the stairway, the concrete floor met an unfinished cement wall.

Karina gasped. Lining the walls all around her were deep wooden shelves. And piled on the shelves were guns. Dozens of them.

Behind her Caleb gave a long, low whistle. "Would you look at that? It's like al Qaeda's storage shed."

She followed Mason into the room and stood in the center, circling to take in the view. How many guns were there? She couldn't begin to count them.

Mason approached a shelf and bent close, his hands clasped behind his back. "AK-47s here." His gaze slid to the shelf next to it. "And M-4s."

"Wow."

Karina turned at Caleb's exclamation to find him examining a heavy-looking weapon with a barrel a couple of inches wide.

"Do you know what this is?" Tones of awe sounded in his voice. "It's an M203 single-shot 40 millimeter grenade launcher."

Mason shook his head slowly, his gaze circling the room. "Can you imagine any reason why a law-abiding citizen would need to own a grenade launcher?"

"Not a single one."

Karina's nerves went taut. Was that a noise upstairs? She tilted her head sideways, listening, but heard nothing else. Maybe it was her imagination. A nervous buzz tingled along her muscles.

"We've seen what we need to see." She covered the two steps between her and Mason quickly and grabbed his arm. "Let's leave and call someone. Detective Grierson maybe."

Mason looked at her for a moment, then nodded. "I'll call Parker and have him meet us in the parking lot." He slipped his phone out of its holder and glanced at the screen. "No service. Let's get out of—"

His voice fell silent when the floor above them

eaked. He and Caleb both ducked, their gazes fixed
n the ceiling. This time Karina was sure. Someone
as upstairs.

Her lungs froze. She scanned the room for a place
• hide. Nothing. Terror gripped her throat and
queezed as feet appeared on the stairs. Shiny, highly
olished shoes. Gray slacks with a pressed seam.

Mason and Caleb both stepped in front of her,
hielding her from the newcomer. Her instinct was
• cower behind them, but she couldn't bear to close
er eyes to the oncoming danger. Her hands on the
aistband of Mason's jeans, she extended her neck
nd peeked over his shoulder.

A relieved breath flooded her lungs as the person
ho descended the stairs came into view. First she
aw a police uniform. Thank goodness! The police
ad arrived! Then the man's face became visible and
he almost laughed with relief. Parker Harding, the
ery person they were going to call.

But he was not alone. Four sets of feet followed
osely on his heels, and before Parker had even
ached the bottom of the stairs, the men came
ito full view. And each one of them was holding
wicked-looking rifle, the barrels pointed her way.

She felt the muscles in Mason's spine stiffen be-
eath her fingers.

"Parker. I was getting ready to call you."

Tension squeezed Mason's voice so tight it almost
queaked. Caleb's hand reached behind his back to-
ard her, and Karina grasped it with one of hers.

"Really? Well, that would have been an interestir conversation." Parker's foot left the last stair, and h stepped aside so the others could move off the stai way. "I see you've stumbled on our little cache."

"Your cache?" Mason's steady voice belied th tremble she felt in his body. "You mean Maddox cache, don't you?"

Parker chuckled. "One and the same, partner." Th chuckle ended abruptly. "Don't tell me you hadr figured it out. I thought for sure Graham said som thing to you."

A puzzle piece fell into place, and Karina swa lowed a gasp. Parker was working with Maddox this weapon scheme. Officer Graham suspected hir and had been trying to warn Mason when he wa killed. That meant—

"You killed your own partner." The accusation sh from her mouth before she could stop it.

Parker's chuckle cut off abruptly. "I had no choic He was on to me." His stare at Mason hardened. "I told you, didn't he? I could tell he was going to lunch yesterday."

Mason shook his head. "No, Parker. He didn't."

The man reared backward as though slapped. The he seemed to recover. "Well, he would have if he lived."

Thoughts of Officer Graham's wife and childre threatened to overwhelm her, but Parker interrupte with a barked order.

"How did you track us here?" Mason asked.

"Mason, Mason. Didn't your mother teach you to close the door when you come into a room? In this case there's a trigger in the doorjamb. After two minutes a silent alarm alerts the security company." His gun barrel jerked toward the stairs. "Upstairs, all of you. There's someone who wants to talk to you."

One of the hardest things Karina had ever done was follow Mason up those stairs. Caleb moved behind her, and his presence provided a barrier between her and the guns of the silent men who moved at Parker's barked command.

They returned to the fitness center's main workout area to find the lights still off, the room still dark. But now a man sat on the abduction machine, a commanding presence in a light gray suit and flanked by a pair of bodyguards who equaled Caleb in size.

Russell Maddox.

Maddox smiled as they came into view.

"Mr. Sinclair, what a surprise to see you again so soon."

Mason felt Karina's body trembling behind him. Even Caleb, ever a tower of strength, hesitated at the top of the stairs.

Maddox completely ignored Karina and Caleb. His sharp gaze caught Mason's and held it.

Where he found the strength to speak, Mason didn't know. "Maddox, the only thing that surprises me is that you bothered to come here and risk exposure. After all, you've worked so hard to distance yourself from this operation. I'm flattered."

Maddox snorted. "Don't be. I'm not here for you. Believe it or not, you've happened to stumble onto a critical meeting for our organization."

The information filtered into his brain. Why would Graham pick tonight to reveal his suspicions? Why would Grierson advise they retreat to a safe location tonight, of all nights? Obviously both of them suspected something, and were moving to stop a critical exchange of some sort. Which meant tonight was not a normal night.

Reasons filtered through his mind.

He took a stab. "Liquifying your assets, I assume?"

Maddox's smile deepened. "It's good to see you've kept your wits sharp during the past four years. Yes, tonight an important exchange will occur." He waved a hand to encompass the gym. "This place has served its purpose. It's time to move on."

Parker took a few steps forward to stand beside Maddox, his gaze fixed on Mason's face. Disgust churned in Mason's stomach at the sight of his smug, arrogant smirk. Whatever role he filled in Maddox's organization, he was responsible for Graham's death. For that alone Mason would like to see that expression wiped clean on a patch of rough concrete.

"You should have stayed gone, buddy." His eyes flickered to a place behind Mason, where Karina stood. "Let the kid take the fall. What difference would it make? Where do you think a poor kid without parents is gonna end up anyway?"

Realization dawned. "You killed José." He spat the accusation. "That's why Alex wouldn't rat you out. He was afraid, because he didn't want to go up against a cop."

Parker tilted his head forward in acknowledgment. "If the kid had just kept his head down and cooperated like we told him, it would have come out okay. The judge would have given him a light sentence. Navarro and Judge Wilkinson would have seen to that."

Behind him Karina gasped. "You've paid a lawyer and a judge?"

Maddox held up a hand, his expression hard. "Enough. We have a meeting to attend, and I don't want to be late. You and you." He pointed out two of the armed men who stood silent guard over them. "Come with me. Harding." His head turned slightly, though his gaze never left Mason's face. "Take the trash out, would you?"

Parker stiffened. "But I thought I was going to the—"

"Do it."

Parker fell silent. Maddox's voice left no room for argument.

The man rose from the machine with a grace that came from hours in the gym. Mason stiffened as he approached and thrust his face within inches of his.

"For what it's worth, I disliked giving the order about your wife. But she was too nosy for her own good." His gaze slid behind Mason, to where Karina stood trembling. "I dislike nosy women."

The floor tilted upward as Mason's head spun. This...this *thug* had given the order to kill Margie? He launched himself after the man's back, but found his arms caught up in a couple of iron grips. The men who'd accompanied Parker down the stairs to the weapons storage room.

Maddox's chuckle trailed after the arms dealer as he left the building.

TWENTY-FOUR

"I can't believe you three are causing me to miss the biggest deal in two decades."

Parker sat twisted around in the front passenger seat of the minivan, his service revolver lying casually across his lap, his glare fixed on Mason. For two cents and a plug nickel, Mason would have launched himself off of the bench seat toward the guy. What stopped him was the presence of a goon with the barrel of his rifle pointed at him, Karina and Caleb. And even worse, his fancy cell phone lay in the console between the driver and passenger seat, the power shut off.

Caleb broke his long silence with a question. "What's so special about tonight? I'll bet there've been a bunch of deals in the years you've been involved with Maddox in this gun scheme."

A wide grin spread across Parker's face. "Very good. You have a brain hiding somewhere beneath all that hair. Yes, I've seen my share of deals in the past *five* years."

His gaze slid to Mason. Parker had been involved

with Maddox since their first year on the force. Since before Margie's death.

Acid surged into his throat. "You…" He thought of about a zillion unflattering terms, but hated to use them because Karina was in the car. "You were in cahoots with Maddox all along."

Parker's smile became frosty. "Very good, Mason. It only took you four years to figure that one out. Yes, I started working with Maddox a few months before Margie's death. In fact, I met with him the morning she discovered the panel in the mirror." The smile faded a fraction, and his eyes glazed. "I hated pulling the trigger, really. But it was my first job, my proving ground."

Acid surged in Mason's stomach, and his head went light. Parker, his own partner, had killed his wife? Bile threatened to choke him. Hatred swirled crimson in his brain. If he could lay hands on the guy…

A soft hand rested on his arm, and a heavy one on his shoulder. With an effort Mason pulled back from the abyss into which his thoughts had threatened to pull him. He placed a hand over Karina's, and turned a grateful gaze over his shoulder toward Caleb.

Having delivered his blow, Parker turned around in the front seat and fell silent.

The van sped eastward, toward the dark, jagged horizon of the Sandia Mountains. They passed the exit for the Sandia Peak Tramway, and continued up the winding road into the foothills and beyond.

Mason kept his gaze fixed outside, on the dark tree-lined landscape that sped past. Sometime during the drive Karina's hand slid down his arm and her fingers entwined his. Behind him he heard the almost imperceptible drone of Caleb's voice, and knew that the big man was praying. Though Mason had had no use for prayer in years, the thought comforted him.

After what seemed like hours in the silent van, the vehicle pulled off the pavement onto a dirt path. They bumped and jolted their way over a winding trail, dark trees looming over them. With every yard Mason's hope dipped lower. They were so far away, how could anyone ever find them?

Finally the vehicle rolled to a stop.

"Well, here we are." Parker's voice held a fake light tone. "End of the line, folks. Everybody out."

He exited the van and the side panel door slid open. For one second Mason considered rushing him, barreling out of the seat and bowling him over, gun or no gun. But the presence of the assault rifle aimed at the back of his head stopped him.

He climbed out of the van and turned to help Karina. Their feet crunched on dried leaves and twigs covering the soft ground.

Parker and the two armed men forced them to walk into the deep tree line. Mason went first, almost feeling his way in the darkness. His feet crashed through the upward sloping underbrush like a thunderstorm in the silent mountain air. It didn't matter. There was nobody within miles to hear. He came upon a small clearing and stepped out of the darkness into a circle of moonlight.

"That's far enough." Parker's voice preceded him from the cover of the forest.

Mason turned slowly, Karina and Caleb lining up beside him. The two goons took up stances on either side of Parker. Mason exchanged a glance with Caleb, and saw no hope in the big man's face.

"So tell me what's special about tonight." Mason didn't really give a flip, but the longer he kept Parker talking, the longer they lived.

Parker studied him for a moment. White moonlight turned his face deadly pale, like a zombie, but his eyes were shrouded in shadows. Finally he nodded. He slid his Glock back into its holster—what did he need it for, when the hoodlums on either side of him had AK-47s trained on their captives—and hooked his thumbs in his utility belt.

"Why not? You can't stop it now. Maddox is selling out. Seems a few folks on the force have gotten a little too curious." His lips thinned with a cold smile. "Yes, Graham was one. That's why I had to take him out. I knew he was zeroing in on me. In fact, I'm pretty sure he was going to clue you in earlier this evening. Are you sure he didn't mention me?"

Mason's mouth went dry. So he hadn't been the target after all. Graham had been. "No. He didn't mention you."

That took the wind out of Parker's sails. He went

till for a moment, but then recovered. "I must have gotten there just in time, then."

Beside him Karina's bare feet shuffled in the cold underbrush. Mason gave her a sympathetic look, but what could he do? They were all about to die in a few minutes.

Caleb's head faced him. At this angle, moonlight illuminated his features. Mason's gaze connected with his, and the guy's eyebrows shrugged sideways.

What? What's he trying to say?

He didn't dare acknowledge, but blanked his expression. Again the eyebrows shrugged sideways, and this time Mason noticed a nearly imperceptible shrug of the massive shoulders in the direction of Parker. Caleb's feet were turned at an unusual angle to his body, pointing toward their captors.

Realization dawned.

He wants to rush them.

Was he crazy?

Mason's thoughts whirled. He had to keep Parker talking while he considered Caleb's silent suggestion.

"What about Grierson? Is he on to you, too?"

Parker laughed. "You tell me. Has he said anything to make you think so?"

Just a warning to get out of the apartment tonight.

"No. I just wondered how much hot water you're in."

Parker's weapon is holstered. If we time a rush just right, we might be able to knock those two off their feet before he can draw his pistol.

"Oh, not much. I've worked for the guy for fiv years, and he's never picked up on a thing. But yo never know. Maddox says we've pushed our luck a far as we should. After tonight there won't be an evidence left."

Mason's gaze connected with Caleb's. He gave very, very slight nod, and saw his friend's lips curve into a grim smile.

Keep Parker talking. "Why? What's going on to night? You leaving town or something?"

"Oh, no. No need for that. Maddox is getting ou of the business. There's a big deal going down. In fact, some very important people are in town from Mexico City." He made a show of pushing the but ton on his watch to illuminate the face. "Right now in fact, they're at the old asylum, making the fina trade. Remember that place?"

Mason knew it. A deserted insane asylum woul be the perfect place for a deal like that to go down.

Parker continued. "Oh, I'm sure they're going t try to convince Maddox to stay in operation. It's bee a lucrative business, after all. It paid off my house an built me a nice little nest egg that makes the polic department's retirement fund look like..." His hea moved as his gaze circled the clearing. He smiled "A pine needle in the forest."

While Parker talked, Mason positioned his fee and shifted his weight for a quick take-off. He locke onto Caleb's gaze in his peripheral vision, his eyes o their captors. When Parker's head swept upward, th armed men on either side of him followed his gaze. Their heads both tilted upward. Just for a second, but that was all they needed.

Mason jerked his head, giving Caleb the signal. They both sprang forward. The big man flew across the small clearing with a speed that belied his size, and Mason did his best to keep up. Then he lost track of Caleb when his head crashed into the hard obstacle of an arm and a gun barrel. There was a disorienting moment when the man lost his balance and sprawled backward, and Mason almost went with him. But he regained his footing at the last moment, and instead of falling full-length on the man, he bent his leg. His knee landed with a sickening and satisfying thud in the man's Adam's apple. While his would-be attacker gasped for breath, Mason snatched the rifle out of his hands and in a single fluid gesture, whirled to point it toward Parker.

But he was too late. Parker's instincts were at least as sharp as his. His former partner had not only unholstered his weapon, but he'd lunged forward and grabbed Karina as well. He stood with one arm across her throat, and the barrel of his Glock pistol pointed at her temple.

For one moment Karina thought she was going to die. She had been stunned into inactivity when both Caleb and Mason sprang forward. If she'd known, she would have moved at the same time. But by the time she realized, she was a fraction of a second too late. She tried to whirl and run, but her bare foot trod on something sharp, and the pain doubled her over. And then Parker's arm was around her neck, and he jerked her upright. She felt the cold metal of his gun press against her temple.

He spun her around, where she came face to face with Mason and Caleb. Both had overpowered their men, and clutched rifles in their hands. Mason's eyes were black orbs in his face. She saw Caleb's lips move in a short prayer, and recognized the words. *Dear Jesus, help her.*

Yes. Please!

She couldn't put together a more eloquent prayer, because the gun pressed against her skull drove out coherent thought.

"Stupid move, Mason."

Parker's voice came from so close that she felt his breath on the crown of her head.

"We both know you're not going to do anything to endanger the girl, so drop your weapons. Both of you."

She stared at Mason, her eyes begging him to… what? What could he do, other than comply?

He reached the same conclusion. His features sagged with defeat and he lowered the weapon.

A chuckle vibrated through her skull from her captor's throat. "I guess this is it, buddy. You should have stayed in Atlanta."

The gun moved away from her head. It swung toward Mason.

No!

Gathering every ounce of strength she could muster, she jerked her head backward and upward. The crown of her skull connected with Parker's chin. Not a stunning blow by any means, but she hoped to at least startle him. At the same moment, she swung her arm out and upward to connect with his. The gun jerked sideways at the same moment an angry curse sounded in her ears.

The weapon exploded. The sound rang in Karina's skull, so loud that for a moment she couldn't see. Then she found herself on the ground in a jumble of arms and legs and bodies. Mason had launched himself toward her, toward Parker, and the impact nearly knocked the breath from her lungs. Fists flew, and she curled herself up into a knot and rolled sideways, out of his way.

"Take that you, you wife killer."

She opened her eyes in time to see Mason's fist connect with Parker's face two times, three, and the man fell back against the ground, unconscious. Relieved tears flooded her eyes. It was over. They'd won.

But then Mason uttered a cry that wrenched at her soul. She sat up as he half ran, half stumbled across the clearing toward Caleb.

The man with the ponytail and a heart of gold lay prone on the ground, blood seeping from a wound in his chest.

TWENTY-FIVE

No. This couldn't happen. He couldn't be the cause of two deaths in one night.

Mason fell to his knees beside his friend, searching his body for signs of movement. "Caleb! Are you alive?"

A frightening amount of blood saturated the front of his friend's denim shirt, flowing from a bullet hole in the massive chest. Behind him he heard Karina's approach, heard her choked voice whispering, "Please, God, save him. Please don't let him die."

Mason jerked Caleb's collar away and placed a finger on the carotid artery. Was there a pulse?

Caleb's eyes did not open, but he spoke. A weak, faint whisper that would have been frightening if Mason hadn't been so glad to hear it. "I'm alive. Don't you dare try mouth-to-mouth on me, Brother."

Mason nearly collapsed with relief. He forced a laugh for the big man's benefit. "Trust me, I don't want that any more than you. Are you going to be okay?"

Caleb gave a weak, shallow cough, and

when he did the blood welled from his wound. "I know where I'm going, and who's waiting there to welcome me home."

The words slapped at Mason. "Don't talk that way, okay? You just hang on, you hear? I'm going to get you out of here."

Karina's prayer gained volume, boosted by a soft sob. "Please, Lord, touch Your son right now. Don't let him die, Father. He has more to do for You here."

Mason left her beside him and ran across the clearing to Parker's unconscious form. Radio, radio. Where was the police radio? He searched the utility belt but found nothing, not even a cell phone. Apparently Parker had removed his radio to do his dirty work.

Parker moaned, and his left hand twitched upward toward his rapidly swelling nose. In another few minutes he would regain full consciousness. Mason searched the heavy utility belt and found his cuffs. Roughly and unceremoniously, he shoved Parker over and cuffed his hands behind his back. There. That would slow him down, anyway. He scooped up the gun on his way to the first of the two thugs. Still unconscious, but for how long? A quick search of the men's pockets revealed no cell phone, but something almost as good. The keys to the van.

He jerked upright. "Karina. Go to the car. Get my cell phone."

He tossed the keys in her direction, and then returned to his task of securing all the weapons before any of their captives regained consciousness.

Karina's bare feet pounded over the debris covering the forest floor. Brittle twigs poked into her arches, once so painfully that she cried out. The ground was cold, so cold, but she couldn't think about that. The hillside sloped downward into impenetrable darkness. Her foot caught on a fallen branch and she went down on her hands and knees, her palms bruised and scraped. She prayed as she ran, but her prayers had been reduced to one single, urgent plea.

"Lord, please, please, don't let him die."

Even though she ran as fast as her bare feet and unfamiliar territory would allow, the journey to the van seemed to take three times longer than when they'd walked the other way. Had she taken a wrong turn? It would be easy to get lost in this pitch blackness. Surely she'd gone too far.

Finally she stumbled from the thick trees onto a dirt road. Panic threatened for a moment. Where was the van? But then her gaze fell on it, about a hundred feet to her right. She'd gone slightly wrong, but at least she'd found it.

The driver's door was unlocked. No need for the key after all. She scooped up Mason's cell phone from the center console, and examined the hillside down which she'd just run. Driving the van to Caleb would be impossible. The trees pressed too closely together. She'd have to return on foot.

Within seconds she was back in the forest, running up the side of the mountain as quickly as she could force her abused feet to go. On the way she fumbled with Mason's phone, and finally pressed the right button on the thin edge. The power-on musical tone almost made her cry with relief.

She took a few precious seconds to stop for a frantic examination of the screen. The indicator was in the top left corner, just like her phone, and it showed full access. *Thank You, Lord!* After a few fumbling attempts she managed to find the previously dialed number, and punched it. Then she took off again, the phone held to her ear. When the line rang, the tone sounded loudly from the speaker. Apparently she'd pressed the speaker button by accident.

A sleepy male voice answered. "Dude, are you kidding? It's five o'clock in the morning."

"This isn't dude, it's me." Her breath came heavy and fast, but not as fast as the adrenaline-fueled thoughts that zipped through her brain. With the huffing and puffing, this guy would probably think she was an obscene phone call if she didn't talk fast.

"I'm Karina Guerrero, and I'm a friend of Mason's. Caleb has been shot and he's bleeding and talking about Heaven and we need help." A sob choked off her rapid-fire monologue.

The voice on the other end became instantly alert. "Where are you?"

"We're up in the Sandia Mountains outside of Albuquerque. A dirt road. We passed the tram on the way, but I don't know where it is, or how far we went beyond it."

A loud shuffling and the voice spoke urgently. "Caleb's been shot. Start praying."

"I have been," she sobbed.

"That's good," the man said, "but I was talking to my wife. I'm going to my computer now, and it'll just take a minute to track you. My name is Brent, by the way. And you're Karina?"

"Yes."

Her breath was starting to come hard in her chest with the effort of running uphill. Had she gone astray? Where was that clearing?

"Karina, you say Caleb's been shot. Where? Is he conscious?"

A branch scraped across her face as she ran by, and she almost dropped the phone. "In the chest. He was conscious about ten minutes ago, but I had to get the phone to call you. He was bleeding a lot."

"Is Mason okay?"

"Yes, but there were three men and they all had guns, and one's a cop, and he's back there with them." She was handling this badly, but she couldn't help it. She couldn't find them. Wait! What was that up ahead? A lighter spot in the darkness which might be the clearing.

"Oh, thank You, Lord." She nearly sobbed with relief. "I found them."

"All right. My computer's up and I'm fixing on your location now."

She crashed into the open to find Mason standing beside Caleb's prone form, an assault rifle pointed at their three captors. Parker and one of the other men had awakened, and were sitting on the ground, watching him warily. She almost threw her arms around Mason in relief, but there was no time. Instead she told him, "I've got your friend in Atlanta on the phone."

Mason expelled a breath, but the grim expression did not leave his face and his eyes did not flicker away from his charges even for a second. Karina dropped to her knees beside Caleb, frantically searching his body for movement.

His chest rose with a shallow breath.

"He's still breathing," she sobbed into the phone.

"Thank the Lord," came Brent's answer on the other end. "I've got a fix on you. I'm going to contact the police."

Mason spoke up, the gun still trained on Parker. "Brent, it's Mason. We need a medical chopper up here first. Caleb's bad. And then contact the FBI. Tell them to get a team over to the deserted insane asylum on the corner of Edith and Osuna because there's an illegal arms deal going down right now. If they're quick they're going to hook a couple of whales."

Karina glanced at Parker, but then looked away quickly from the pure hatred she saw in his face.

They listened to the conversation as Brent, using another phone, relayed their location and the rest of the information in staccato. Minutes passed. Sirens breathing continued to be shallow and rapid, and he did not open his eyes. Karina kept her hand on him, so if he was aware he would know he wasn't alone. Tears streaming down her cheeks, she whispered the Psalm she would want to hear if she were in his place.

"The Lord is my shepherd; I shall not want. He maketh me to lie down in green pastures."

Finally a sound reached the clearing. Faint at first but growing rapidly louder. It was a sound that made her want to weep with relief. The sound of an approaching helicopter.

TWENTY-SIX

The bright lights of the hospital corridor blinded Mason when he and Karina stepped from the helicopter pad into the building. Blinking, he kept his hand on the stretcher rail and ran to keep up with the paramedic's pace.

"You hold on, Caleb. Do you hear me? I don't want your death on my hands, okay?"

He caught Karina's gaze across the stretcher. Tears flowed unchecked down her face. With his free hand he brushed moisture from his own cheek. Caleb couldn't die. He just couldn't.

A couple of nurses and a white-coated doctor joined their sprint down the hallway. They reached a double door at the end, and one of the nurses dashed forward to slap a button on the wall. As the doors fanned open, the other said, "I'm afraid you can't go any farther. You'll find the waiting room back that way. The doctor will talk to you once he's stable."

Mason nodded, and stopped.

"Wait." The command, though faint, was clearly audible. Amazingly, Caleb's hand rose. "Mason."

The paramedics hesitated, and Mason rushed forward. He bent over the stretcher and looked into his friend's pale face. A hazy gaze met his.

"Do you have a prayer in you, Brother?"

Mason sent a frantic glance in Karina's direction. "He wants you to pray."

"No." The words came in a whisper. "I want *you* to."

It had been years since he'd prayed. Four, to be exact. But what could he do, say no to his dying friend? Irritation flashed through him. Leave it to Caleb to force a man to pray.

Mason grabbed the hand that lay at Caleb's side, and bowed his head. "Dear Father, please watch over Caleb and keep him safe. Guide the doctors and give them the skill they need. Protect my friend's life, even though I think he's a dirty rat for tricking me into praying at the one time he knows I won't refuse. Amen."

A slight smile hovered about lips that were only a few shades darker than the sheet on which he lay. "Amen. That wasn't so bad, was it?"

"No, it wasn't so bad." Mason found himself blinking back a fresh batch of tears. Actually it had felt kind of good. But he wasn't about to admit that. He squeezed Caleb's hand one last time. "Be safe, my friend."

The stretcher was whisked away, and the doors closed behind it. Karina slipped both arms around his waist. He closed his eyes and pulled her close. Now the long wait began.

And since he'd broken the ice, he might as well try another prayer or two.

Over the next three hours Mason had the opportunity to use his prayer muscles, and found that they hadn't atrophied as much as he'd feared. But as the wait stretched on, the more anxious he grew. What was taking so long?

When the blond doctor they'd seen earlier stepped into the waiting room, he and Karina were off their chairs like a shot.

"How's my friend?" He winced at the demanding tone, but the woman didn't seem to mind.

Her smile was weary. "It was touch and go there for a while, but he's finally stable. The bullet nicked his right lung and lodged dangerously close to his spine, but we were able to get it before it caused any permanent damage."

Mason's muscles didn't relax so much as wilt.

Karina threw her arms around him and hugged. "Thank God."

"He's going to be in recovery for several hours, so why don't you go get some rest? You both look like you've had a long night."

Which was the understatement of the year, but Mason was suddenly too weary to do more than nod. "Thank you, Doctor."

When she left the waiting room, she passed a

familiar figure in the doorway. Grierson. The skin
sagged around his eyes, and his shirt looked like it
had been wadded into a ball and shoved in a corner
for a week. But one glance at the satisfaction in his
grim smile told Mason all he needed to know.

"You got Maddox."

"Oh, yeah. And a paddy wagon full of others, too,
including the biggest cartel boss we've ever landed."

"Cartel?" Karina tilted her head. "Maddox was
dealing in guns *and* drugs?"

Grierson nodded. "The two go hand-in-hand
lately." His gaze slid to Mason's. "You almost blew a
twenty-four month operation, Sinclair. When I heard
you were in town, I should have followed my first instinct to lock you up to keep you out of our way until
this thing was over."

"So you knew about Maddox all along?"

"Oh, yeah. Harding too." His smile went hard.
"Can I tell you how good it felt to nail him?" He
turned to Karina. "Which reminds me, ma'am. Your
brother will probably be released in another hour or
so. The feds are prepared to drop all charges related
to his activity with the sale of illegal weapons in return for his eyewitness testimony regarding Harding
shooting that poor kid."

Karina's eyes closed, and she blew out breath.
"Thank goodness."

"Of course he'll have a chance to talk to another
attorney, a clean one this time."

"I knew it." Mason straightened, and cast a

triumphant glance at Karina. "Navarro was on Maddox's payroll."

"And the D.A. has a feeling he's going to sing, too."

Karina looked surprised. "The D.A. isn't crooked, then?"

"Oh no, ma'am. He'd been helping us build our evidence file from the very beginning. He suspected Navarro but couldn't be sure until he presented his request to try your brother, a fourteen-year-old kid, as an adult. That had to be a move orchestrated by Maddox."

Her jaw went slack. "I had no idea."

Mason couldn't let an I-told-you-so moment pass. "Next time listen to me. Which reminds me." He gathered his brow into a scowl and turned it on his former boss. "You could have told me about Parker. I might have been able to help."

"Graham wanted to, but I preferred to keep you out of it. You're a civilian now."

"So Graham was working with you?" Mason had a hard time speaking the man's name without an accompanying wave of grief. He'd misjudged a good man.

"From early on. I assigned them as partners so he could gather evidence from the inside. Speaking of partners." Grierson's head ducked and he averted his eyes for a moment. When he looked back up, he held Mason's gaze steadily. "I was wrong about you back when your wife died. I'm sorry."

The sting of tears behind his eyes surprised Mason.

Until he heard the words, he'd had no idea how much healing they would bring. He blinked hard, to keep them at bay while he stuck out his hand and shook Grierson's.

"Thank you. I appreciate that." The warmth of their grasped hands melted away the last of the four-year-old ice buried in Mason's soul.

Then Grierson straightened. "I've got to get out of here. I've got a mountain of paperwork before I can get any sleep." He started to leave, and then turned back with a piercing gaze. "That reminds me. You got that report I asked for, Sinclair?"

Mason grinned. "Still working on it, *Detective*."

The man smiled and left the room chuckling.

What had started out to be a day of death was turning into one of healing. And once the process of healing old wounds had begun, Mason wanted to keep going until there were none left. Until all the ghosts had been laid to rest.

He turned to Karina, but couldn't quite meet her gaze. "You know, since he started the apology thing, I owe you one. Or maybe several."

"Mason." She laid a hand on his arm. "After everything you've done for Alex and me, you don't owe me anything."

"Yes, I do." The touch of her fingers on his felt so good, so right. Moving almost instinctively, he slipped an arm around her waist. "I should never have hurt you the way I did. I'm sorry."

"It's okay," she whispered. "You were in love."

Her lips trembled. He found himself unable to look away from them. How many times had he felt those silken lips moving against his?

"I was in love with Margie." Speaking her name didn't hurt like it would have a week ago. He *had* loved Margie, in a different way. But Margie was gone, and for the first time, he felt like he could look ahead to a future without her.

Without her. But not without Karina.

He ducked his head and sought her eyes so she could read the truth in his. "But now, I'm in love with you."

The fluorescent light in the waiting room turned the sudden tears that flooded her eyes into diamonds. Her hand slid up his arm and around his neck.

"You are?"

Was that joy he heard in her voice?

"I am." He tightened the arm around her waist and pulled her close. "And I was wondering if maybe, if you've forgiven me for breaking your heart, you might let me try to put the pieces back together."

In answer, she rose up on her bare toes, pulled his head down toward hers and swept him into a kiss that left no doubt that she had, indeed, forgiven him.

EPILOGUE

Karina slid a platter of steaming tortillas onto the table. "Now you'll get to taste some real Mexican food, just the way my *abuela* used to fix it."

Her new friend Lauren turned from the counter in Mason's small kitchen with a bowl of rice and beans. "I hope you like it, baby," she told her husband, "because I've been trained by an authentic Mexican cook, and I'm eager to try out my new skills solo."

Brent, seated in a chair pushed against the wall, rubbed his hands together. "It smells great."

At one end of the table Caleb extended his neck toward the dish piled high with *carne asada* and inhaled with obvious pleasure. "Bring it on, Sister. I've been injured, you know. Got to keep up my strength."

Karina smiled. The big man had said that at every meal in the two months since she and Alex arrived in Atlanta. Either she was a really good cook, or he was one hungry man.

Brent rolled his eyes expansively. "It's been almost six months since your surgery. Don't you think you're pretty much healed?"

Caleb shook his head. "As long as these two beautiful ladies keep producing home-cooked meals like this one, I'll play that card as long as it lasts."

Karina lifted her head toward the connecting doorway to the living room. "Mason and Alex, come and eat before it gets cold."

"Coming!"

The sound of scuffing feet on carpet preceded them, and then they appeared, jostling each other like two kids to see who could arrive first. Karina's stomach fluttered at the sight of Alex, laughing with the man who had reclaimed her heart. Alex slid into his chair with a victorious grin, but Mason came to her. He slid an arm around her waist and pulled her close for a kiss.

Oh, how she loved this man! Their shared secret made the kiss even sweeter. They weren't quite ready for a public announcement, but soon they'd share their news with their friends. How fun it would be to proclaim their upcoming wedding. But for now it was a tender, private treasure between the two of them.

"Don't you two ever get tired of kissing?" asked Alex in teenager disgust.

Mason released her, but his gaze continued to caress hers. "Never."

"You know," said Caleb as they took their places around the table, "we ought to consider changing our name from F.A.S.T. to something else. We seem to be just as good at matchmaking as we are at helping people falsely accused of a crime." He looked point-

edly at Lauren and Brent, and then at Mason an
Karina, then assumed an injured air. "What I can'
understand is how you two ended up with the beau
tiful women. After all, I'm the best of the bunch."

Everyone laughed, and Mason said, "Tell you wha
The next pretty girl who calls for help is all yours."

"I'll take her. Now." His gaze swept the laden table
"Who wants to pray over our meal?"

Mason spoke up immediately. "I will."

Karina exchanged a smile with Caleb. What
change God had made in this man.

She bowed her head and closed her eyes. Beneat
the table Mason's hand sought hers. With a full hear
she laced her fingers in his, and whispered a praye
of her own.

*Thank You, Lord. You've given me everything
ever dreamed of.*

* * * * *

ar Reader,

few months before I began writing *Bullseye,* I saw
ews article about a raid on a cache of illegal weap-
s stored in a secret room behind the mirrors in a
me gym. Oh, the possibilities for a fiction writer! I
uldn't resist taking that idea and expanding it into
tory. Of course, I moved the gym from Mexico
Albuquerque, and invented a whole cast of suspi-
us characters. That's the way stories are born, at
st in my mind.

Mason's character was a challenge. He first ap-
ared in *Dangerous Imposter,* and in that book his
arp sarcasm made him a terrific sidekick. But as a
o? I wanted you to like him, and sarcasm can so
en make someone appear harsh. I needed to show
sensitive side, even though he would never reveal
imself. So I had to make him vulnerable, and to do
t he had to experience some pain. Sorry, Mason!
least his story has a happy ending.

hope you enjoyed reading *Bullseye,* the second
ok in the Falsely Accused miniseries from Love
pired Suspense. As I pen this letter, I'm working
the plot for the third and final book in the series.
ope you're looking forward to Caleb's story as
ch as I am!

'd love to hear what you thought of my book. Con-
t me through www.VirginiaSmith.org, or become

my friend on Facebook at facebook.com/ginny.p.sm
Or you can write to me at Virginia Smith, P.O. B
70271, West Valley City, Utah, 84170.

Virginia Smith

Questions for Discussion

1. Did you believe Alex when he adamantly denied involvement with a street gang? Why, or why not?

2. Karina feels responsible for her brother getting involved in José's murder. Is she?

3. What impact does Karina and Mason's failed romance play on their relationship as they try to clear Alex's name?

4. Why does Karina staunchly refuse to let Mason sleep on her couch, even with a locked door between them?

5. Can you identify the role each of the three members of the Falsely Accused Support Team play in solving the crime in *Bullseye?*

6. Mason decides to take a head-on approach with Russell Maddox and confronts the man in his office building. Was this a wise decision or a rash one?

7. Whom did you suspect of killing José at various points in the story?

8. Mason bases a lot of his impressions on body

language. Do you think it's possible to understand people based on their body language? Can you give an example of when someone's body language has communicated a different message than their words?

9. Both Karina and Mason receive healing during the story. Identify the source of pain for each of them, and how their healing came about.

10. What is the turning point in Karina's feelings for Mason?

11. Mason does not trust Hector from the beginning. Why does he form such a negative opinion of him?

12. In fact, Mason distrusts just about everything— Hector, Maddox, Graham, Grierson. Why do you think he is so suspicious of everyone?

13. What was Caleb's reason for requesting that Mason pray for him before he is wheeled into surgery?

14. With which character in *Bullseye* did you most identify? Why?

LARGER-PRINT BOOKS!

GET 2 FREE
LARGER-PRINT NOVELS
PLUS 2 FREE
MYSTERY GIFTS

Love Inspired.
SUSPENSE
RIVETING INSPIRATIONAL ROMANCE

Larger-print novels are now available...

LARGER-PRINT BOOKS!

**GET 2 FREE
LARGER-PRINT NOVELS
PLUS 2 FREE
MYSTERY GIFTS**

Larger-print novels are now available...

YES! Please send me 2 FREE LARGER-PRINT Love Inspired® novels and my 2 FREE mystery gifts (gifts are worth about $10). After receiving them, if I don't wish to receive any more books, I can return the shipping statement marked "cancel". If I don't cancel, I will receive 6 brand-new novels every month and be billed just $4.99 per book in the U.S. or $5.49 per book in Canada. That's a saving of at least 23% off the cover price. It's quite a bargain! Shipping and handling is just 50¢ per book in the U.S. and 75¢ per book in Canada.* I understand that accepting the 2 free books and gifts places me under no obligation to buy anything. I can always return a shipment and cancel at any time. Even if I never buy another book, the two free books and gifts are mine to keep forever.

122/322 IDN FEG3

Name _____ (PLEASE PRINT) _____

Address _____ . _____ Apt. #

City _____ State/Prov. _____ Zip/Postal Code

Signature (if under 18, a parent or guardian must sign)

Mail to the **Reader Service:**
IN U.S.A.: P.O. Box 1867, Buffalo, NY 14240-1867
IN CANADA: P.O. Box 609, Fort Erie, Ontario L2A 5X3

Not valid to current subscribers to Love Inspired Larger-Print books.

**Are you a current subscriber to Love Inspired books
and want to receive the larger-print edition?
Call 1-800-873-8635 or visit www.ReaderService.com.**

* Terms and prices subject to change without notice. Prices do not include applicable taxes. Sales tax applicable in N.Y. Canadian residents will be charged applicable taxes. Offer not valid in Quebec. This offer is limited to one order per household. All orders subject to credit approval. Credit or debit balances in a customer's account(s) may be offset by any other outstanding balance owed by or to the customer. Please allow 4 to 6 weeks for delivery. Offer available while quantities last.

Your Privacy—The Reader Service is committed to protecting your privacy. Our Privacy Policy is available online at www.ReaderService.com or upon request from the Reader Service.

We make a portion of our mailing list available to reputable third parties that offer products we believe may interest you. If you prefer that we not exchange your name with third parties, or if you wish to clarify or modify your communication preferences, please visit us at www.ReaderService.com/consumerchoice or write to us at Reader Service Preference Service, P.O. Box 9062, Buffalo, NY 14269. Include your complete name and address.

LILP11B